BBC CHILDREN'S BOOKS

UK | USA | Canada | Ireland | Australia
India | New Zealand | South Africa

BBC Children's Books are published by Puffin Books,
part of the Penguin Random House group of companies
whose addresses can be found at global.penguinrandomhouse.com.

www.penguin.co.uk   www.puffin.co.uk   www.ladybird.co.uk

First published 2017
001

Written by Justin Richards and Jon Green
Part of this text was previously published in an abridged format in *Doctor Who: The Essential Guide*, 2013
Illustrations on page 133 by Stuart Manning, page 191 by Adam Howling,
page 203 by Dan Green and page 205 by John Ross and Alan Craddock
All other illustrations used under licence granted by artists named throughout,
in accordance with Puffin Illustrated Adventures competition (2017) terms and conditions
With thanks to Abigail Horn and Steven Thornton
Copyright © BBC Worldwide Limited, 2017

Printed in China

A CIP catalogue record for this book is available from the British Library

ISBN: 978–1–405–92722–2

All correspondence to:
BBC Children's Books
Penguin Random House Children's
80 Strand, London WC2R 0RL

BBC
DOCTOR WHO

100 ILLUSTRATED ADVENTURES

PUFFIN

A GREAT ADVENTURE IN TIME AND SPACE . . .

For thousands of years, the Time Lord known as the Doctor has been travelling in his TARDIS across the galaxies. From the explosive creation of the Universe until its eventual end, the Doctor has perhaps found himself caught up in more incredible adventures than any other being in the entire history of creation.

Sometimes he might pause for tea. Occasionally he finds time to read. He's even been known to go fishing for Gumblejacks. But while other life forms might find these activities fulfilling, the Doctor is never happier than when he's caught up in the most thrilling and dangerous adventures you can imagine.

Never happier, and never more brilliant.

The Doctor has had so many adventures that they would never fit into a single book like this. (Unless that book was somehow bigger on the inside than the outside . . . but that's impossible, isn't it?)

In these pages, you'll find just one hundred of the Doctor's most wonderful, jaw-dropping and eye-popping escapades, from the First Doctor to the Twelfth Doctor and every Doctor in between.

These adventures have been illuminated with stunning illustrations from the Doctor's fans themselves, entered in response to the *Illustrated Adventures* competition held by Puffin Books in 2017. The art collected here showcases a wealth of creative talent and reminds us why Earth has always been one of the Doctor's favourite planets.

If you enjoy reading these stories, then rest assured: there are many more adventures to hear about, and many more adventures yet to come . . .

1
An Unearthly Child

An adventure for: First Doctor, Susan, Ian and Barbara
First shown: 23 November–14 December 1963 (4 episodes)
Written by: Anthony Coburn

Two of the teachers at Coal Hill School – Ian Chesterton and Barbara Wright – are concerned about one of their pupils. Susan Foreman seems incredibly clever and knowledgeable in some areas, like history and science, but her knowledge of some basic facts is strangely lacking. She even thinks that Britain uses a decimal system for currency!

Ian and Barbara follow Susan home, and find that she apparently lives with her grandfather in a junkyard. Worried for Susan's safety, Barbara and Ian force their way inside a police telephone box where they believe the old man, who calls himself the Doctor, is keeping Susan.

The police box is actually a TARDIS – bigger inside than out, and capable of travelling through time and space. Despite Susan's assurances, the Doctor insists he can't let the teachers leave as they will bring future knowledge to the present day now they have seen inside his TARDIS.

The TARDIS dematerialises and takes the Doctor, Susan, Ian and Barbara back in time on Earth. Suddenly finding themselves in prehistoric times, the travellers are captured by a primitive tribe that has lost the secret of fire. They must work together to negotiate with the cave people if they are to have any hope of escape . . .

RIGHT: Illustration by Kevin Parrish

2 The Daleks

An adventure for:	First Doctor, Susan, Ian and Barbara
First shown:	21 December 1963–1 February 1964 (7 episodes)
Written by:	Terry Nation

The TARDIS lands on the planet Skaro, in the middle of a petrified jungle. The ground is ash, and the trees brittle stone: the result of a terrible nuclear war. The Doctor and his companions discover a vast metal city and encounter the Daleks for the very first time.

Survivors of the nuclear conflict, the Daleks now live inside protective survival machines within their metal city. Their machines pick up static power from the metal floors, so the Daleks cannot leave the city. They send Susan out to take a message to the Thals – their opponents in the war, now mutated into humanoids.

The Thals give Susan anti-radiation drugs that will cure her and her friends, who are all suffering as a result of radiation left from the war. In return, Susan tells the Thals the Daleks are offering them food and supplies. But this is a trap – the Daleks' only interest in the Thals is their total extermination.

The Doctor and his friends escape the Dalek city, and warn the Thals of the impending danger. Together, they lead an attack on the Dalek city and manage to destroy its power source – disabling the Daleks before they can flood the atmosphere with more deadly radiation.

ABOVE: Illustration by Ian Wells

RIGHT: Illustration by Wayne Whited

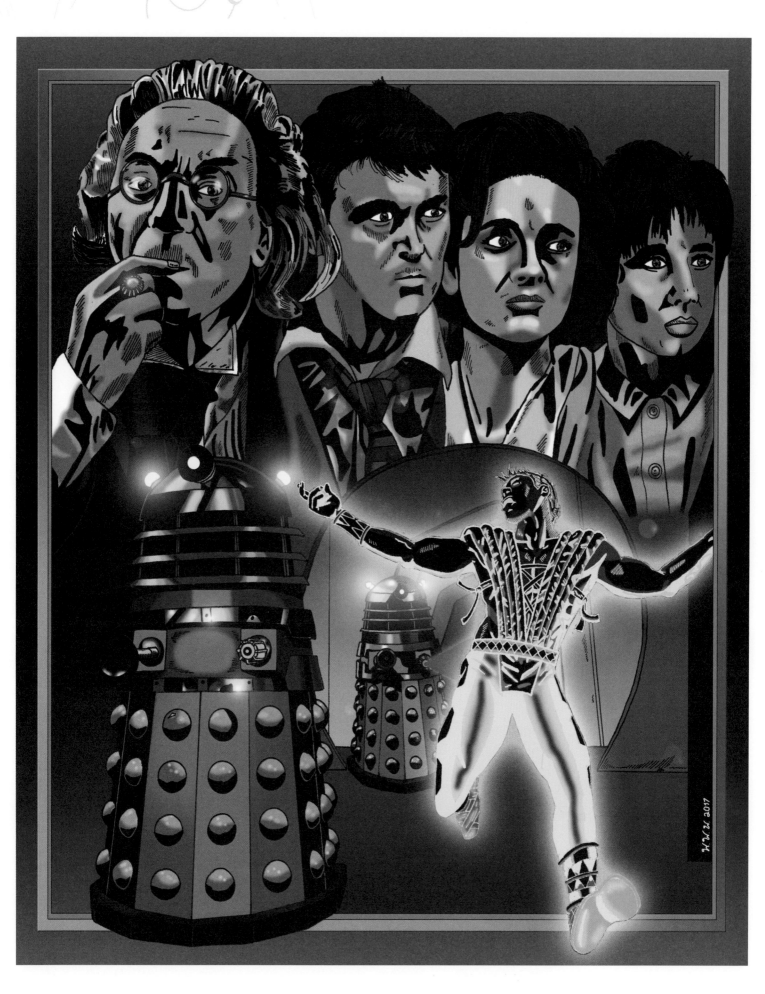

3
The Time Meddler

An adventure for: First Doctor, Vicki and Steven
First shown: 3–24 July 1965 (4 episodes)
Written by: Dennis Spooner

The TARDIS lands on a beach in north-east England in 1066, close to where Viking invaders will come ashore before King Harold of England defeats them at the battle of Stamford Bridge. The Doctor, Vicki and their new friend, Steven, soon discover that they are not the only time travellers present . . .

They encounter a monk in an otherwise abandoned monastery. The 'monk' has a gramophone player, a small stove for cooking, a wristwatch . . . and a TARDIS! He is a time meddler from the Doctor's own race, the Time Lords, who plans to destroy the Viking fleet before it lands. That way, he reasons, King Harold won't have to fight them. He will then be able to face William the Conqueror with fresh, rested troops and win the Battle of Hastings. The meddling monk thinks that Harold being king would be far better for the future of western civilization.

Despite the monk's attempts to imprison them, the Doctor and his companions thwart his scheme. The Doctor sabotages the monk's TARDIS, removing the dimensional controls so it's no longer bigger on the inside and trapping the Time Meddler in 1066.

ABOVE: Illustration by Jessica Ramage

RIGHT: Illustration by Luke Joyce

4
The Daleks' Master Plan

An adventure for: First Doctor, Steven and Katarina
First shown: 13 November 1965–29 January 1966 (12 episodes)
Written by: Terry Nation and Dennis Spooner

The TARDIS brings the Doctor, Steven and Katarina, their new Trojan companion, to the planet Kembel. Steven has blood poisoning, and the Doctor sets off to find medicine to cure him. What he doesn't know yet is that elsewhere on the planet, the Daleks are forming an alliance with other alien races . . .

Mavic Chen, the traitorous Guardian of the Solar System, has provided the Daleks with the Taranium core of their most deadly weapon yet: the Time Destructor. The Doctor manages to steal the vital core and escapes in Chen's spaceship with security agent Bret Vyon.

With the Daleks in pursuit, Katarina bravely sacrifices her own life to save her friends. Vyon is also killed, and the Daleks now chase the Doctor, Steven and tough security agent Sara Kingdom through time and space. After a battle among the pyramids of ancient Egypt, the Doctor is forced to hand over the core.

Back on Kembel, the Daleks turn on their former allies, including Chen, and prepare to activate the Time Destructor. The Doctor is able to turn it against the Daleks, but tragically kills Sara Kingdom in the process, who is caught in the weapon's destructive field.

RIGHT: Illustration by Logan Koontz

5
The War Machines

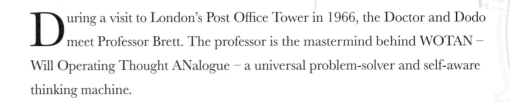

An adventure for:	First Doctor, Dodo, Ben and Polly
First shown:	25 June–16 July 1966 (4 episodes)
Written by:	Ian Stuart Black

During a visit to London's Post Office Tower in 1966, the Doctor and Dodo meet Professor Brett. The professor is the mastermind behind WOTAN – Will Operating Thought ANalogue – a universal problem-solver and self-aware thinking machine.

There are plans to network WOTAN with major computers across the globe. However, WOTAN starts taking control of the humans working on the project, including Professor Brett. It programs them to build War Machines, militarised mobile computers, which WOTAN plans to use to take over Earth.

Polly, Brett's secretary, and her friend Ben, a young merchant seaman, are captured, but Ben escapes and tells Sir Charles Summer, the senior civil servant overseeing the project, what is going on. With the Army defenceless against the War Machines, the Doctor captures one, and reprograms it to destroy WOTAN.

Now back in her own time, Dodo decides to stay on Earth. The Doctor prepares to leave aboard the TARDIS alone, but just before it dematerialises Polly and Ben follow him inside.

RIGHT: Illustration by Richard W. Taylor

6

The Tenth Planet

An adventure for:	First Doctor, Ben and Polly
First shown:	8–29 October 1966 (4 episodes)
Written by:	Kit Pedler and Gerry Davis

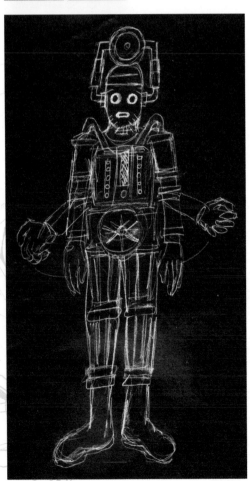

ABOVE: Illustration by Francis McHardy

The TARDIS arrives in 1986 at the coldest place on Earth, close to the International Space Command Snowcap Base in Antarctica. The base is monitoring a manned space flight when a new planet appears – a planet that looks very much like Earth.

It is Earth's lost twin planet, Mondas, home of the Cybermen. The Cybermen are humans who have gradually replaced their bodies with artificial limbs and organs made of metal and plastic. They have also altered their brains so that they are now logical beings with no emotions at all.

Mondas is absorbing energy – draining it away from Earth. A group of Cybermen take over Snowcap Base, aiming to use a powerful Z Bomb to destroy Earth before Mondas absorbs too much energy.

Ben discovers the Cybermen are vulnerable to radiation, and the crew of the base defeat the Cybermen there. With the bomb disarmed, Mondas explodes and the Cybermen remaining on Earth collapse and die.

The Doctor also collapses, his elderly body exhausted and worn out. As Ben and Polly watch in amazement, he miraculously changes into a new form . . .

ABOVE: Illustration by Connor Adkins

7

The Power of the Daleks

An adventure for:	Second Doctor, Ben and Polly
First shown:	5 November–10 December 1966 (6 episodes)
Written by:	David Whitaker and Dennis Spooner

The TARDIS brings the newly regenerated Second Doctor to the human colony planet of Vulcan. Here he is mistaken for an Examiner, sent from Earth to inspect the colony. With Polly and Ben, the Doctor sets about 'inspecting' Vulcan and finds a crashed space capsule that a scientist named Lesterson has recovered from a mercury swamp. To his horror, the Doctor finds two deactivated Daleks inside.

Lesterson has already removed a third Dalek and given it the power it needs to become active. The Doctor tries to warn everyone that the Daleks are dangerous, but the Daleks pretend to be helpful, servant-like robots, keen to aid the colony and perform menial tasks.

In fact, the Daleks are biding their time while they siphon off energy to power a huge Dalek production factory hidden inside their spaceship! A group of rebels tries to use the Daleks to help them take control of the colony, but they're too late – the Daleks are ready to emerge in force and exterminate everyone.

The Doctor manages to turn the Daleks' power source against them, destroying the creatures and saving the day. But just as the TARDIS leaves, the eye-stalk of an apparently dead Dalek lifts to watch it go.

RIGHT: Illustration by Richard Young

18

8
The Moonbase

An adventure for:	Second Doctor, Ben, Polly and Jamie
First shown:	11 February–4 March 1967 (4 episodes)
Written by:	Kit Pedler

In AD 2070, the Doctor, Ben, Polly and Jamie arrive on the Moon, where they find a weather control station. The base is run by a man called Hobson and his deputy Benoit. Members of the base's crew are falling victim to a mysterious disease. Investigating, the Doctor discovers that the epidemic is the result of a toxin that has been released by the Cybermen.

The Cybermen intend to take control of the station's crew and use the base's gravity-generating weather control device, the Gravitron, to radically alter Earth's weather, thereby destroying the planet. Realising that the Cybermen's chest units are made of plastic, Polly leads the fightback by spraying them with chemical solvents.

The first wave having been defeated, more Cybermen advance across the Moon's surface. However, the Doctor determines that the alien cyborgs are vulnerable to gravity fluctuations. Hobson uses the Gravitron device against them, sending the Cybermen and their landing craft deep into space.

RIGHT: Illustration by Paul Duncan

9
The Evil of the Daleks

An adventure for:	Second Doctor, Jamie and Victoria
First shown:	20 May–1 July 1967 (7 episodes)
Written by:	David Whitaker

The Doctor and Jamie McCrimmon are in London in 1967 when they see the TARDIS being driven away on the back of a lorry. They trace it to an antiques shop, where all the Victorian antiques are genuine, but somehow appear brand new. They arrange to meet the owner, Edward Waterfield, but are gassed into unconsciousness . . . and wake up later to find themselves in a country house in the year 1867, owned by Victorian scientist Theodore Maxtible.

This is all part of a Dalek plan to synthesise the 'Human Factor' – the essence of what makes a human – so they can understand why humans have defeated them so many times. The Daleks cruelly force the Doctor to test Jamie, recording his emotions and reactions when he tries to rescue Waterfield's daughter, Victoria, from the Daleks. From this, they plan to distil the Human Factor.

On Skaro, the Dalek Emperor reveals that the Doctor has actually helped to distil the 'Dalek Factor' – the impulse to exterminate – which the Daleks will now spread through Earth history. But the Doctor 'infects' some Daleks with the Human Factor and they begin to question the orders of their leaders. With a Dalek civil war raging, the Doctor, Jamie and Victoria escape in the TARDIS.

RIGHT: Illustration by Paul Carey

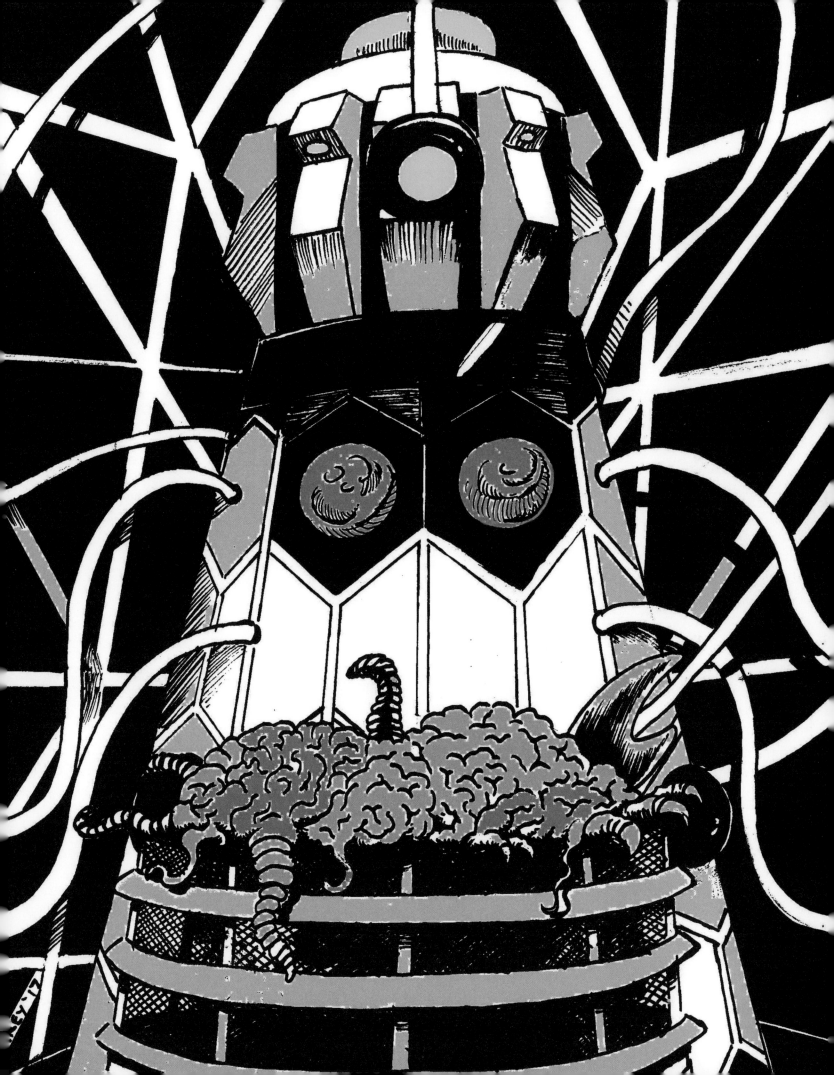

10
The Tomb of the Cybermen

An adventure for: Second Doctor, Jamie and Victoria
First shown: 2–23 September 1967 (4 episodes)
Written by: Kit Pedler and Gerry Davis

The TARDIS arrives on the planet Telos, just as human archaeologist Professor Parry is trying to lead an expedition through the entrance doors to a gigantic buried city. Parry is searching for the ancient lost remains of the legendary Cybermen – Telos was their home planet. The expedition is being funded by Kaftan and her colleague Klieg, members of the super-intelligent Brotherhood of Logistics. With help from the Doctor, the locked doors to the city are prised open.

But the Cybermen are not as extinct as was thought. They are in fact frozen, in huge honeycomb-like tombs in caverns beneath the city. Kaftan and Klieg are secretly planning to revive the Cybermen and work with them to conquer humanity. Klieg revives the Cybermen, but soon discovers that they have ideas of their own . . .

The Doctor traps the Cybermen below the city, but they dispatch deadly Cybermats to attack him in the control room. They also convert Toberman, Kaftan's servant, so that he is part-Cyberman. But when the Cyber Controller then kills Kaftan, the still-loyal Toberman turns on the Cybermen instead. The Doctor reprograms the city's computer systems to seal the Cybermen back in their tombs, and the Controller is electrocuted and destroyed.

The Doctor tells Jamie that he thinks the Cybermen are defeated for good – but doesn't spot one small Cybermat as it wriggles away . . .

RIGHT: Illustration by Finn Clark

11
The Ice Warriors

An adventure for: Second Doctor, Jamie and Victoria
First shown: 11 November–16 December 1967 (6 episodes)
Written by: Brian Hayles

As a new ice age grips the Earth of the future, humanity battles to hold back the glaciers using ionisation devices. At Brittanicus Base, the ioniser is barely coping. The Doctor, Jamie and Victoria arrive in the snowy wastelands of Earth, just as an ancient warrior is found encased in ice and excavated from the glacier.

But the warrior isn't just a large man, or some ancient human chieftain, as the scientists at the base believe. He's an alien from Mars whose ship was caught in the glacier millennia ago.

Revived, Varga the 'Ice Warrior' kidnaps Victoria and awakens his ship's crew. Brittanicus Base commander, Leader Clent, is warned that continuing to use the ioniser could cause the Martian's spaceship to explode and contaminate the whole area.

Meanwhile, the Ice Warriors realise that, after so long, their own world must be long dead, so Varga decides that they will make Earth their new home planet.

Taken prisoner by the Ice Warriors, the Doctor eventually gets the upper hand and takes control of their ship and its sonic weapons, forcing them to retreat. Clent risks using the ioniser as a weapon, stopping the ice flow and destroying Varga and his warriors together with their ship.

RIGHT: Illustration by Jonathan Savage

12

The Web of Fear

An adventure for: Second Doctor, Jamie and Victoria
First shown: 3 February–9 March 1968 (6 episodes)
Written by: Mervyn Haisman and Henry Lincoln

The TARDIS is caught in space, held tight by a mysterious web. The Doctor manages to break free and the TARDIS lands in a tunnel of the London Underground. The Doctor, Jamie and Victoria soon find that the city is deserted – London has been evacuated after a strange mist appeared above ground, forming 'webs' in the tunnels beneath the city.

The Doctor's old enemy the Great Intelligence is back, and once again using robot Yeti servants to do its bidding. Jamie, Victoria and the Doctor meet up with Travers – who helped defeat the Intelligence forty years ago – and his daughter Anne, who are working with the military. The army is led by Colonel Lethbridge-Stewart.

The Great Intelligence has been waiting for the Doctor – it plans to drain his mind, using a special machine to take his knowledge and experience. As Jamie manages to get control of one of the Yeti, the Doctor sabotages the machine so that it will instead drain the mind of the Great Intelligence. Unfortunately, before the machine can complete its task, the Doctor is 'rescued' by his friends – and the Intelligence escapes once more.

RIGHT: Illustration by Gareth Thomas

13
The Invasion

An adventure for: Second Doctor, Jamie, Zoe and UNIT
First shown: 2 November–21 December 1968 (8 episodes)
Written by: Derrick Sherwin

The Doctor, Jamie and Zoe accidentally arrive inside a secure area owned by a company called International Electromatics. They are picked up by the military and taken to their old friend Alistair Lethbridge-Stewart – now a brigadier, in charge of the newly formed UNIT organisation. UNIT is investigating International Electromatics – the world's biggest electronics manufacturer – and its enigmatic managing director, Tobias Vaughn.

The Doctor discovers that Vaughn is in league with the Cybermen, who are planning an invasion. Cybermen are being shipped to Earth deactivated in protective cocoons, then awakened at IE's warehouses and distributed through the London sewers ready to take over. A hypnotic signal is then transmitted through the micromonolithic circuits present in all of IE's products. Earth is soon paralysed, and the Cybermen emerge from the sewers to invade . . .

Breaking into the IE Building, the Doctor persuades Vaughn to help him defeat the Cybermen. Zoe helps the RAF destroy the Cyber fleet by calculating missile firing patterns – then, finally, UNIT manages to redirect a Russian missile to destroy the main Cyber ship. The ship explodes, along with the huge Cyber-megatron bomb it is carrying.

RIGHT: Illustration by Alexis West

14
The War Games

An adventure for: Second Doctor, Jamie and Zoe
First shown: 19 April–21 June 1969 (10 episodes)
Written by: Terrance Dicks and Malcolm Hulke

The TARDIS arrives in the middle of the First World War – or so it seems. Before long, the Doctor is accused of being a German spy and sentenced to be shot by firing squad. Things soon become even more strange when the Doctor is then saved by a redcoat soldier from the eighteenth century! Next, before they know it, the Doctor, Jamie and Zoe are being charged at by Roman soldiers . . .

The Doctor and his friends are not on Earth at all, but in the middle of 'war games' – re-enactments of Earth wars organised by an alien War Chief. With the help of a rogue Time Lord, the aliens are using the war games to select the best soldiers from Earth, the most aggressive planet in the galaxy. They will form these soldiers into a huge, brainwashed 'super army', charged with enforcing peace across the entire galaxy.

The Doctor defeats the aliens, but the only way he can think of to get the thousands of stranded humans home is by calling on the help of his own people – the Time Lords – but they capture him and put him on trial for interfering in other planets and times. The Time Lords wipe Jamie and Zoe's memories of all but their first adventure with the Doctor and send them home.

The Time Lords then decide that, as he has shown a liking for the planet, the Doctor's punishment should be exile to Earth in the twentieth century. They give him a brand-new appearance, while also taking away the expertise he would need to escape in the TARDIS . . .

RIGHT: Illustration by
David Checkley

15
Spearhead from Space

An adventure for: Third Doctor, Liz and UNIT
First shown: 3–24 January 1970 (4 episodes)
Written by: Robert Holmes

Exiled to Earth in the twentieth century by the Time Lords, the Doctor arrives in the TARDIS and immediately falls unconscious. His arrival coincides with a strange meteor shower that is being investigated by UNIT.

The recovering Doctor soon meets his old friend Brigadier Lethbridge-Stewart. Together, they discover that the Nestenes are planning to invade, replacing senior politicians and military figures with Auton duplicates. Killer Autons – deadly plastic mannequins – have been distributed to shops across the country.

As the invasion begins and the Autons attack, the Doctor and UNIT infiltrate the plastics factory where the Nestenes are based. Their leader, Channing, is creating a monstrous plastic creature that will house the bulk of the Nestene Consciousness as they take over the planet. As UNIT battles the Autons, the Doctor and his new assistant, scientist Liz Shaw, manage to destroy the creature, and the Nestenes withdraw . . .

The adventure ends with the Brigadier now accepting that the Doctor is really who he claims to be, despite looking completely different, and the Doctor agrees to work with UNIT for the foreseeable future.

RIGHT: Illustration by Claye Hodge

16
Inferno

An adventure for:	Third Doctor, Liz and UNIT
First shown:	9 May–20 June 1970 (7 episodes)
Written by:	Don Houghton

UNIT is involved with security at the Inferno Project, where Professor Stahlman's team is attempting to drill through the Earth's crust to extract Stahlman's gas – a potential new energy source. But workers at the project are infected with a green sludge that turns them into aggressive creatures, the Primords . . . Even Stahlman himself is infected!

Trying to use the project's reactor to help repair the TARDIS, the Doctor is accidentally transported sideways in space and time to a parallel world, where Britain is a fascist state. Here, everyone is different – in keeping with the very different world around them. The Brigadier is the sadistic and cowardly Brigade Leader, and Liz Shaw is not a brilliant scientist, but a soldier.

In this world, the Inferno Project is running ahead of schedule. The Primords are running amok, killing everyone in their path. The drills penetrate the Earth's crust, prompting earth tremors and volcanic eruptions capable of destroying the world . . .

The Doctor manages to escape back to his dimension just in time to close down the Inferno Project before the catastrophe is repeated.

RIGHT: Illustration by Freya Dowell

17
Terror of the Autons

An adventure for:	Third Doctor, Jo and UNIT
First shown:	2–23 January 1971 (4 episodes)
Written by:	Robert Holmes

An old adversary of the Doctor's – the Master – arrives on Earth. He is in league with the Nestenes and has devised a plan for them to invade. The Master steals and reactivates a Nestene energy globe from their first failed invasion (see *Spearhead from Space*), and takes it to a plastics factory. Here, he hypnotises the owner into helping create more Autons . . .

After experimenting with a deadly plastic armchair and a killer doll, the Master decides that the Nestenes' main weapon of attack will be plastic daffodils. Thousands are given away to the general public, supposedly as a promotion. When they are ready to invade, the Nestenes will activate the flowers, which spray plastic over people's nose and mouth to suffocate them.

The Doctor and his new companion, UNIT trainee Jo Grant, discover the plan – but they are captured by the Master. Meanwhile, UNIT battles against the Autons and the Master prepares to open a link to allow the Nestenes to invade in force. The Doctor and Jo escape, and he is able to persuade the Master that the Nestenes will betray him. Together they eject the Nestenes back into space. The Master escapes to fight another day, but the Doctor has sabotaged his TARDIS so that the Master is stranded on Earth.

RIGHT: Illustration by Andrew Kennedy

18
The Sea Devils

An adventure for: Third Doctor and Jo
First shown: 26 February–1 April 1972 (6 episodes)
Written by: Malcolm Hulke

The Doctor and Jo visit the Master, who is being held in a high-security prison on an island. While they are there, they discover that ships have been mysteriously sinking in the local waters. Right at the centre of the sinkings is an abandoned sea fort, which is being converted into a SONAR test station.

The Doctor and Jo visit the fort, but are stranded there when their boat is destroyed. Then they are attacked by a 'Sea Devil' – an underwater-dwelling type of Silurian.

The Master has tricked his prison governor into allowing him access to special equipment, and has contacted the Sea Devils. They rescue him from prison and capture the Doctor. The Doctor offers to negotiate a peace between the Sea Devils and the human race, but his efforts are disrupted by an attack by the Royal Navy.

As the Master incites the Sea Devils to war and the Navy battles against them, the Doctor is left with no choice but to trick the Master and destroy the colony of Sea Devils entirely, exploding the base by reversing the polarity of the neutron flow.

RIGHT: Illustration by Chris Sick

19
The Three Doctors

An adventure for: Third Doctor, First Doctor, Second Doctor, Jo and UNIT
First shown: 30 December 1972–20 January 1973 (4 episodes)
Written by: Bob Baker and Dave Martin

The power of the Time Lords is being drained away into a mysterious black hole. Their only hope is the exiled Doctor – all three of him!

On Earth, UNIT finds itself besieged by strange gelatinous creatures that also seem to be hunting for the Doctor. The Time Lords bring the first three incarnations of the Doctor together, although they only have enough power to enable the First Doctor to communicate through the TARDIS scanner.

Together, the Doctors realise the 'Gel Guards' have been sent to get the Doctor and take him into the black hole, to a world of antimatter. Here they discover that Omega – the Time Lords' stellar engineer, who provided the power source that gave

them time travel – has survived. Now he wants to escape from the black hole and take revenge on the Time Lords whom he believes abandoned and betrayed him.

In Omega's black-hole world, he can create anything by the power of his will. The Doctors work out that in fact Omega died long ago and only his will still survives, insisting that Omega exists, meaning that he can never leave.

Omega's world is destroyed – and him with it. The Doctors each return to their own times, bidding one another friendly goodbyes. The Third Doctor is delighted to discover that, as a reward for his heroism, the Time Lords have returned his knowledge of how to fly the TARDIS through space and time.

RIGHT: Illustration by Cheyanne Sneade

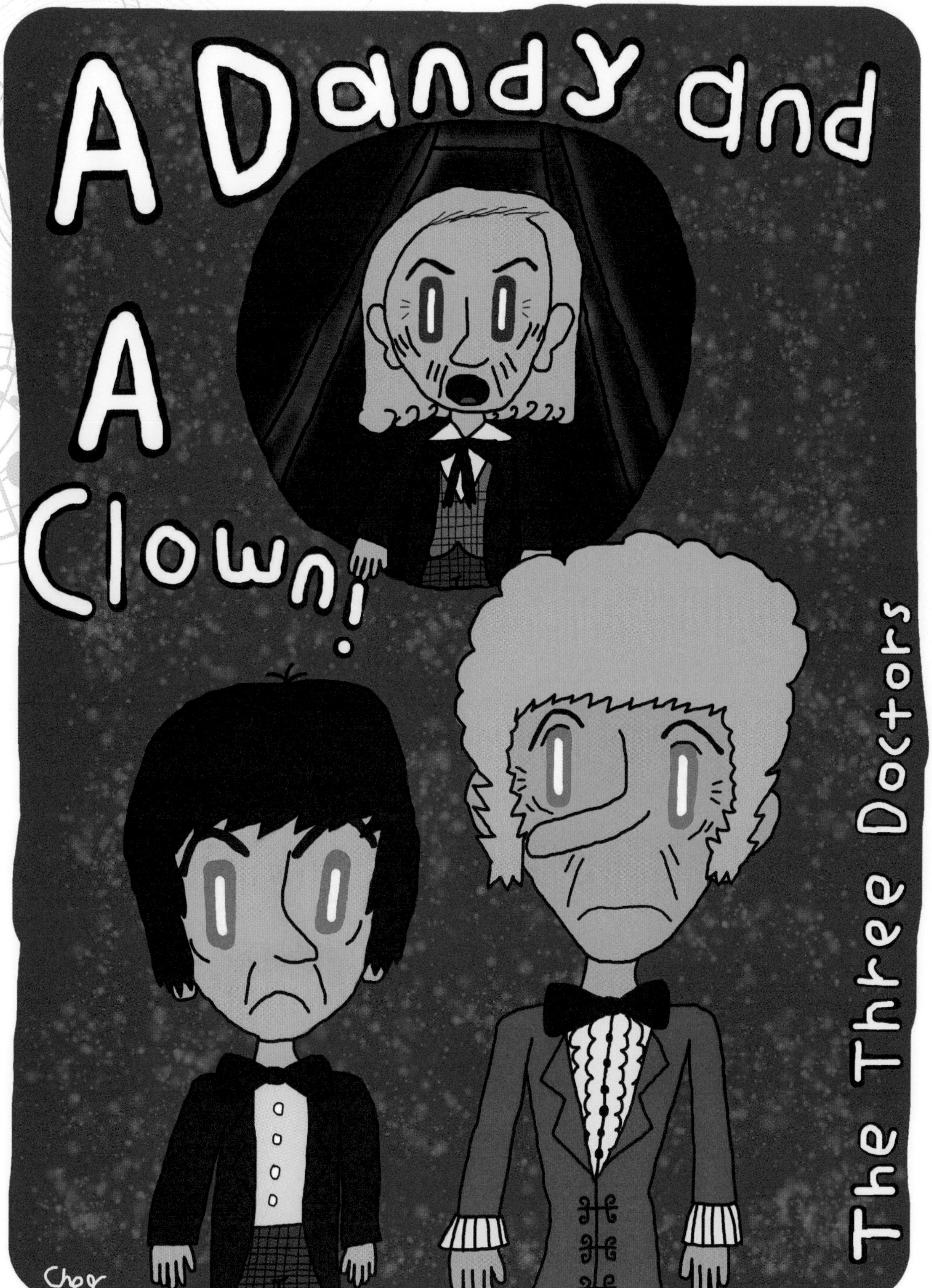
A Dandy and A Clown!
The Three Doctors
Cher

20
The Green Death

An adventure for:	Third Doctor, Jo and UNIT
First shown:	19 May–23 June 1973 (6 episodes)
Written by:	Robert Sloman and Barry Letts

UNIT is brought in after a mysterious death at a disused coal mine, close to the headquarters of Global Chemicals. The chemical company claims to have discovered a way of refining oil with no waste or pollution. But working with a local group of ecologists, the Doctor discovers that the Global Chemicals' process does indeed produce waste, which they have been dumping down the mine. The deadly waste is fatal on contact with the skin and has caused maggots to mutate and grow in size.

UNIT tries to contain a plague of maggots that burrows up from the mine workings. Meanwhile, the Doctor infiltrates Global Chemicals disguised first as a milkman, then as a cleaning lady! There he discovers the real head of Global Chemicals – a megalomaniac computer called BOSS, which has the ability to take over people's minds and is planning world domination.

The Doctor manages to destroy BOSS, but now he has to stop the maggots before they metamorphose into giant flies that spit poisonous chemical waste. With the help of UNIT soldier Sergeant Benton, the Doctor takes a fungus that is deadly to the maggots and scatters it around the mine.

The maggots are defeated, but at a party to celebrate the victory, the Doctor is heartbroken to hear that Jo will no longer be travelling with him – she has fallen in love with scientist Professor Clifford Jones, whom she wants to marry and travel the world with.

RIGHT: Illustration by Paul Carey

21
Planet of the Spiders

An adventure for:	Third Doctor, Sarah and UNIT
First shown:	4 May–8 June 1974 (6 episodes)
Written by:	Robert Sloman and Barry Letts

A large blue crystal – which the Doctor found on Metebelis Three and gave to Jo Grant as a wedding present (in *The Green Death*) – is discovered to be important to a race of giant spiders who live on the planet in the far future.

The spiders determine to get the crystal back, and open a route to contemporary Earth. While Sarah and retired UNIT captain Mike Yates investigate the Meditation Centre where the spiders first appear, the crystal is stolen by Lupton – a human who is in league with the spiders.

The Doctor and Sarah travel to Metebelis Three, where they discover the giant spiders need the crystal to deliver to The Great One. She is an enormous spider, living inside a huge crystal cave under the mountains.

The Doctor confronts the Great One, who is destroyed by the power of the crystal. But the Doctor's body is also massively damaged by the crystal radiation. The TARDIS takes him back to Earth, where he regenerates under the ministrations of another Time Lord – his old mentor, K'anpo – and watched in amazement by the Brigadier and Sarah Jane Smith.

RIGHT: Illustration by Jake Summer

22
Robot

An adventure for:	Fourth Doctor, Sarah, Harry and UNIT
First shown:	28 December–18 January 1975 (4 episodes)
Written by:	Terrance Dicks

Sarah and the Brigadier witness the transformation of the Third Doctor into the Fourth Doctor. The base's medical officer, Harry Sullivan, then takes charge of monitoring his recovery.

Meanwhile, top-secret MoD plans for a disintegrator gun have been stolen. The Doctor joins the UNIT investigation into the theft and discovers that it was the work of a group of dissident scientists that call themselves Think Tank. Meanwhile, Sarah discovers that the thefts are the work of the K1 Robot, the invention of one Professor Kettlewell, originally programmed to be unable to hurt humans.

The director of Think Tank, Miss Winters, ordered that the robot be reprogrammed to steal the means to build the disintegrator gun. She intends to use the weapon to acquire the control codes for the nuclear weapons belonging to the world's superpowers. Think Tank is planning to take over the world, threatening to initiate World War Three to achieve their goal.

Persuaded by Sarah to act with conscience, the robot eventually kills its creator, but suffers a breakdown as a result. It even goes so far as to try to launch the nuclear weapons itself. In an attempt to destroy it using the disintegrator gun, the Brigadier actually infuses it with energy, which makes it grow to a huge size.

To halt its rampage, the Doctor is forced to destroy the machine using a metal virus, hypothesised in Kettlewell's own research notes.

RIGHT: Illustration by Davey Beauchamp

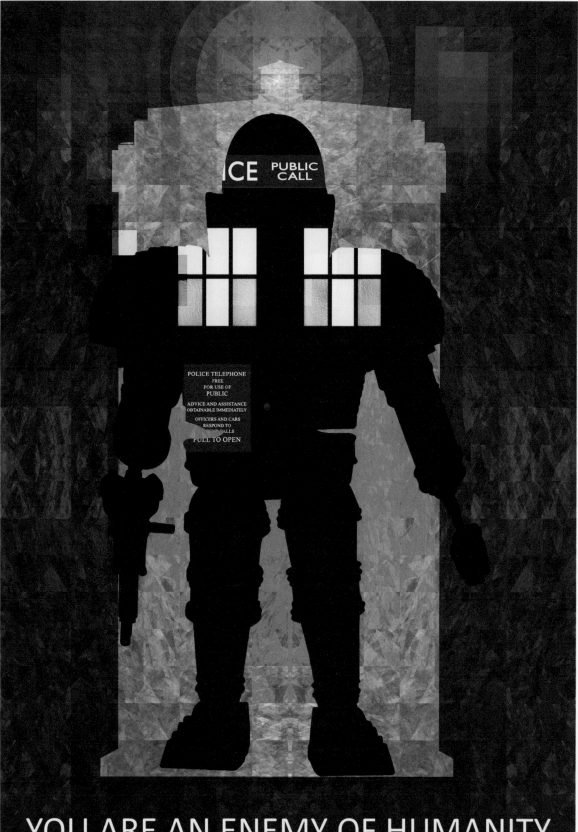

23
The Ark in Space

An adventure for:	Fourth Doctor, Sarah and Harry
First shown:	25 January–15 February 1975 (4 episodes)
Written by:	Robert Holmes

Thousands of years in the future, Earth has been devastated by solar flares. The survivors lie in suspended animation on board Space Station Nerva – nicknamed 'The Ark'. They should have woken centuries ago, but the systems have been infiltrated by a Wirrn Queen. This huge space-travelling insect has sabotaged the station and laid her eggs inside one of the sleeping technicians.

When the Doctor, Sarah and Harry arrive, they reactivate the systems and the humans begin to wake up. But, horribly, not all of them are entirely human any more . . . The Wirrn can absorb not just the bodies of their victims, but their knowledge too. Even Lazar, the commander of the Ark, or 'Noah' as he is known, is infected and begins to change into a Wirrn.

Luckily for the Doctor and his friends, Noah retains a small part of his humanity. The Doctor persuades him to lead the Wirrn swarm away from the Ark in a transport ship, which then explodes.

RIGHT: Illustration by Crina Magalio

24

Genesis of the Daleks

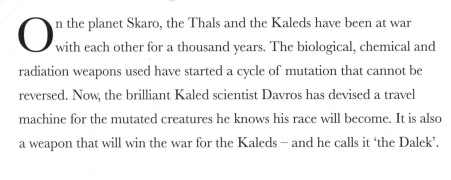

An adventure for:	Fourth Doctor, Sarah and Harry
First shown:	8 March–12 April 1975 (6 episodes)
Written by:	Terry Nation

On the planet Skaro, the Thals and the Kaleds have been at war with each other for a thousand years. The biological, chemical and radiation weapons used have started a cycle of mutation that cannot be reversed. Now, the brilliant Kaled scientist Davros has devised a travel machine for the mutated creatures he knows his race will become. It is also a weapon that will win the war for the Kaleds – and he calls it 'the Dalek'.

The Time Lords have foreseen a future where the Daleks exterminate all other life forms and rule supreme. They send the Doctor, Sarah and Harry to Skaro on a mission to stop the Daleks from ever being created.

While the Doctor is able to slow the process, he cannot stop Davros's Daleks entirely. They all but destroy the Thals, before suddenly turning on their own creator. But the Doctor tells his friends that, while the Daleks will create chaos and terror, many future worlds will become allies just because of their fear of the Daleks. Out of their evil will come some good.

Trapped inside a bunker deep below the surface of Skaro, the Daleks make their plans to emerge and become the supreme rulers of the Universe . . .

RIGHT: Illustration by Allister Simmons

25
Terror of the Zygons

An adventure for:	Fourth Doctor, Sarah, Harry and UNIT
First shown:	30 August–20 September 1975 (4 episodes)
Written by:	Robert Banks Stewart

RIGHT: Illustration by Anthony Wallis

LEFT: Illustration by Leighton Noyes

The Brigadier uses a space–time telegraph to summon the Doctor back to Earth. Oil rigs in the North Sea are being attacked and destroyed, and the Doctor discovers that the culprit is . . . the Loch Ness Monster! A Zygon spaceship crashed into Loch Ness centuries ago, and the crew has remained hidden, depending on the milk of a huge armoured cyborg creature called a Skarasen. It's the Skarasen that has become known to humans as the Loch Ness Monster.

Now, the Zygons have discovered that their home-planet of Zygor has been destroyed. They have started destroying oil rigs as part of a plan to take over Earth as a new home for the Zygon refugees.

The Zygons can make themselves look like captured humans – and even imitate the Doctor's friend Harry. They launch and fly their ship towards London, intent on releasing the Skarasen and destroying an important conference being held there, killing all attendees, including the Prime Minister.

The Doctor manages to destroy the Zygon ship and, with the help of the Brigadier and UNIT, the Zygon warlord Broton is killed before he can summon the Skarasen to continue the attack on London. The Doctor distracts the monster with a signalling device, and with nowhere else to go, the Skarasen heads home to Loch Ness . . .

26
Pyramids of Mars

An adventure for: Fourth Doctor and Sarah

First shown: 25 October–15 November 1975 (4 episodes)

Written by: Stephen Harris (Lewis Greifer and Robert Holmes)

ABOVE: Illustration by Christine Martino

The TARDIS is drawn off course and arrives at Marcus Scarman's house in 1911. Scarman is an Egyptologist, who has been excavating a newly discovered pyramid. But the unlucky Scarman has stumbled upon the tomb of Sutekh, who kills him and uses his animated dead body to carry out his will.

Sutekh is an alien war criminal who was chased to ancient Egypt by his fellow Osirans, led by Horus. He was imprisoned beneath a pyramid in a force field controlled from Mars. The event became the basis for the ancient Egyptian gods and legends. Now, Sutekh is using service robots that look like Egyptian mummies to build a missile to destroy the Eye of Horus – the power source that holds him prisoner.

With the help of Scarman's brother, Laurence, the Doctor and Sarah destroy the missile. But they are captured by Sutekh, who uses the TARDIS to send Scarman to Mars to deactivate the Eye of Horus. The Eye is destroyed, but as Sutekh escapes down a space–time tunnel, the Doctor uses TARDIS technology to move the threshold into the far future, so that Sutekh ages to death before he can escape.

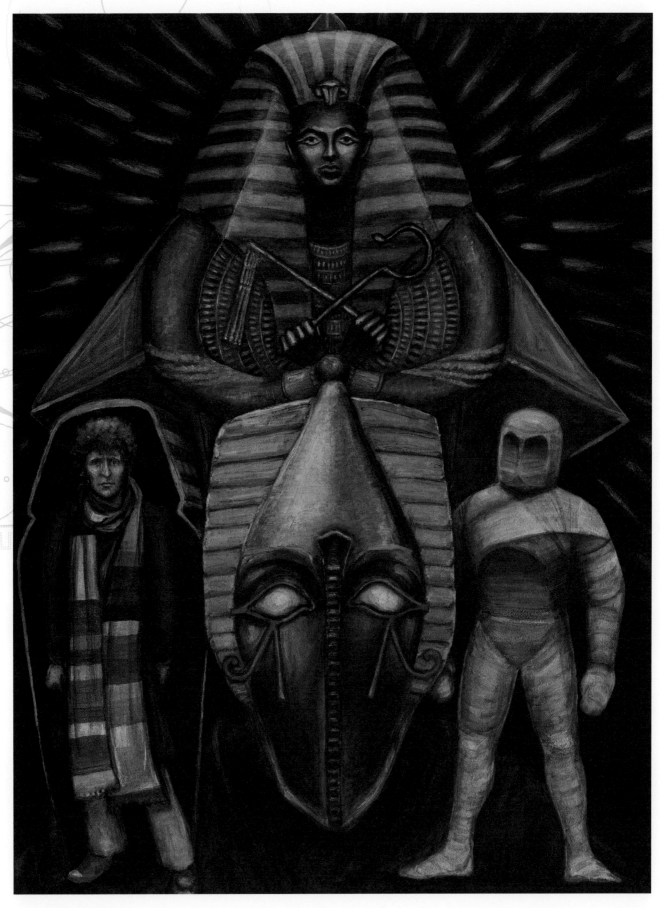

ABOVE: Illustration by Kat Lunoe

27
The Brain of Morbius

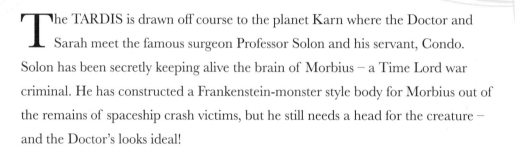

An adventure for:	Fourth Doctor and Sarah
First shown:	3–24 January 1976 (4 episodes)
Written by:	Robin Bland (Terrance Dicks and Robert Holmes)

The TARDIS is drawn off course to the planet Karn where the Doctor and Sarah meet the famous surgeon Professor Solon and his servant, Condo. Solon has been secretly keeping alive the brain of Morbius – a Time Lord war criminal. He has constructed a Frankenstein-monster style body for Morbius out of the remains of spaceship crash victims, but he still needs a head for the creature – and the Doctor's looks ideal!

Solon drugs the Doctor, but before he can operate, the Doctor is taken by the Sisterhood of Karn. The Sisters have great mental powers and live forever because of their Elixir of Life. They think the Doctor is a Time Lord agent sent to steal the Elixir, and decide to burn him at the stake.

The Doctor is rescued by Sarah, but she is temporarily blinded in the process. She regains her sight in time to see the completed Morbius creature stalking her. Solon has completed it with an artificial brain case for a head.

The Doctor manages to convince the Sisters that Solon is resurrecting Morbius, their old enemy. They decide to help the Doctor and Sarah destroy the creature. The Doctor dazes Morbius in a mind-bending contest and then the Sisters drive him over a cliff.

RIGHT: Illustration by Richard Hollingdale

28

The Seeds of Doom

An adventure for: Fourth Doctor and Sarah
First shown: 31 January–6 March 1976 (6 episodes)
Written by: Robert Banks Stewart

The Doctor and Sarah investigate a strange seed pod that has been discovered by a scientific team in Antarctica. The Doctor recognises it as a Krynoid – an alien plant life form that is hostile to all animal life, including humans. The pod infects one of the scientists, who begins to mutate into a Krynoid, but the creature is destroyed when the Antarctic base is suddenly blown up.

The explosion is caused by Scorby, who is working for billionaire botanist Harrison Chase. He manages to get hold of a second pod, and brings it back to England for Chase. The Doctor and Sarah escape the explosion and track down Chase, who captures Sarah and plans to infect her so that he can cultivate a Krynoid for his collection. The Doctor rescues Sarah, but in the fracas, one of Chase's stooges is infected instead.

As the creature grows to gigantic size, it passes its powers on to other plants so that they also become hostile! With every plant turning against them, the Doctor manages to escape and calls in UNIT to destroy the deadly creature. They return to the mansion and the Doctor saves Sarah from Chase, who is then killed in his own composting machine. UNIT manages to destroy the Krynoid just in the nick of time, before it germinates and spreads its seeds across England.

RIGHT: Illustration by Ian Wells

29
The Hand of Fear

An adventure for: Fourth Doctor and Sarah
First shown: 2–23 October 1976 (4 episodes)
Written by: Bob Baker and Dave Martin

Arriving in a quarry, Sarah is trapped by a rockfall. In amongst the debris she finds a stone hand. The hand is the last remnant of Eldrad, an alien who was blown up in a spaceship. Eldrad's life essence is stored in the ring on the hand, and begins to influence Sarah. She takes the hand to a nuclear power station, where it absorbs radiation and comes to life. Eldrad is reconstituted as a beautiful woman made of stone, just like the hand.

The Doctor takes Eldrad back to her own planet, Kastria, where she claims she should be ruler, having been deposed from her throne there by invaders. But Kastria is a dead world, with traps set for Eldrad should she return.

Eldrad is now revealed in his true form as a power-hungry maniac who tried to overthrow the rightful king, Rokon. The Kastrian people destroyed themselves rather than risk Eldrad surviving to return and force them to wage war across the galaxy. Enraged, Eldrad decides to take the TARDIS to Earth to enslave humanity, but the Doctor trips him with his scarf and Eldrad falls into a deep abyss.

Receiving a summons from Gallifrey, the Doctor is obligated to say farewell to Sarah, as he cannot take her to his home planet with him.

RIGHT: Illustration by Anthony Blake

30
The Deadly Assassin

An adventure for:	Fourth Doctor
First shown:	30 October–20 November 1976 (4 episodes)
Written by:	Robert Holmes

The Doctor, travelling alone, arrives back on Gallifrey for the President's resignation – except the Doctor has seen visions of the President being assassinated. He tries to warn the authorities, but becomes a hunted fugitive. When he finally manages to get to the assassin's vantage point above the huge Panopticon, a ceremonial chamber, the Doctor finds he has been set up. The President is killed, and the Doctor is arrested for the crime.

Behind the plot is the Master. He has used up all his regenerations and is close to death – an emaciated, wasted figure. His plan is to use the power of the Eye of Harmony, the centre of a black hole controlled by the President of the Time Lords, to restore his body to health, and framing the Doctor is a bonus.

But the Doctor announces he is standing for the now-vacant post of President, and has to be freed under Time Lord law so he can press his claim. He tracks down the Master's accomplice – Chancellor Goth. Inside the all-powerful Matrix, the Time Lords' store of all knowledge, Goth and the Doctor do battle in a nightmare world created from Goth's will. The Doctor eventually wins, and is able to stop the Master before all of Gallifrey is sucked into a black hole.

RIGHT: Illustration by Carl Dutchin

31
The Face of Evil

An adventure for: Fourth Doctor and Leela
First shown: 1–22 January 1977 (4 episodes)
Written by: Chris Boucher

The TARDIS lands on a mysterious jungle planet where the Doctor is captured by a savage tribe called the Sevateem. The primitives worship a god called Xoanon. The Doctor is denounced as the Evil One of legend, but having survived the Test of the Horda, the Doctor discovers that the Sevateem's god is actually the computer from a spaceship that the Time Lord tried to repair once, long ago. Having reprogrammed it using his own brain patterns, he unintentionally drove the machine intelligence mad, giving it multiple personalities.

While the Sevateem are descended from the spaceship's original survey team, Xoanon is tended to by the Tesh, descendants of the ship's original technicians who have developed destructive psychic powers. With the help of a Sevateem girl called Leela, the Doctor boards the spaceship and deletes the computer's excess personalities. He also succeeds in reconciling the two warring tribes and tells them that Xoanon is cured and now able to support their new society.

As the Doctor heads off on his travels once more, Leela insists on joining him. Even though he refuses, she charges past him into the TARDIS and pushes a button which starts its dematerialisation.

RIGHT: Illustration by Jamie Austin

32
The Robots of Death

An adventure for: Fourth Doctor and Leela
First shown: 29 January–19 February 1977 (4 episodes)
Written by: Chris Boucher

ABOVE: Illustration by Peter Nolan

Storm Mine 4 travels through the deserts of a distant planet collecting mineral ores from the sand. It is run by robots supervised by a small human crew. A Super Voc – SV7 – coordinates the other Voc-class robots as well as the mute, single-function Dum robots. Everyone knows the robots are completely safe – they are programmed not to harm humans. But then one of the crew is found strangled . . .

Arriving in the TARDIS, the Doctor and Leela are the obvious suspects. But the Doctor realises that someone is reprogramming the robots so that they are able to kill. Maniac scientist Taren Kapel has taken the place of one of the crew and is planning a robot revolution.

With the help of D84, a robot detective, the Doctor unmasks Kapel. The converted robots turn on the rest of the crew, and the Doctor and Leela are caught up in a battle to the death.

D84 sacrifices himself to help activate a robot-defeating device of the Doctor's invention – with that device, and the help of a handy helium gas canister, the Doctor and Leela are able to end the robot threat and escape once more in the TARDIS.

RIGHT: Illustration by Andy Lambert

33
The Talons of Weng-Chiang

An adventure for:	Fourth Doctor and Leela
First shown:	26 February–2 April 1977 (6 episodes)
Written by:	Robert Holmes

The Doctor decides to take Leela to the theatre in Victorian London, but their trip is interrupted when they discover a group of Chinese ruffians hiding a dead body. The Chinese men are from the Tong of the Black Scorpion, a secret organisation dedicated to the service of the great god Weng-Chiang.

The Tong is led by stage magician Li H'Sen Chang, who is performing at the Palace Theatre with his ventriloquist's dummy, Mr Sin. But Sin is actually a robot from the far future with the brain of a pig, and is a creature that revels in death and carnage. Both Sin and Chang are working for Magnus Greel – a fifty-first-century war criminal who has escaped to nineteenth-century London and is searching for his lost time cabinet. Horribly deformed, Greel keeps himself alive by extracting the life-essence from young women.

With the help of pathologist Professor George Litefoot and theatre manager Henry Gordon Jago, the Doctor and Leela track Greel to his headquarters, the House of the Dragon. There, they manage to defeat both Greel and Mr Sin, using Greel's own horrible human distillation machine against him.

RIGHT: Illustration by Jake Rowlinson

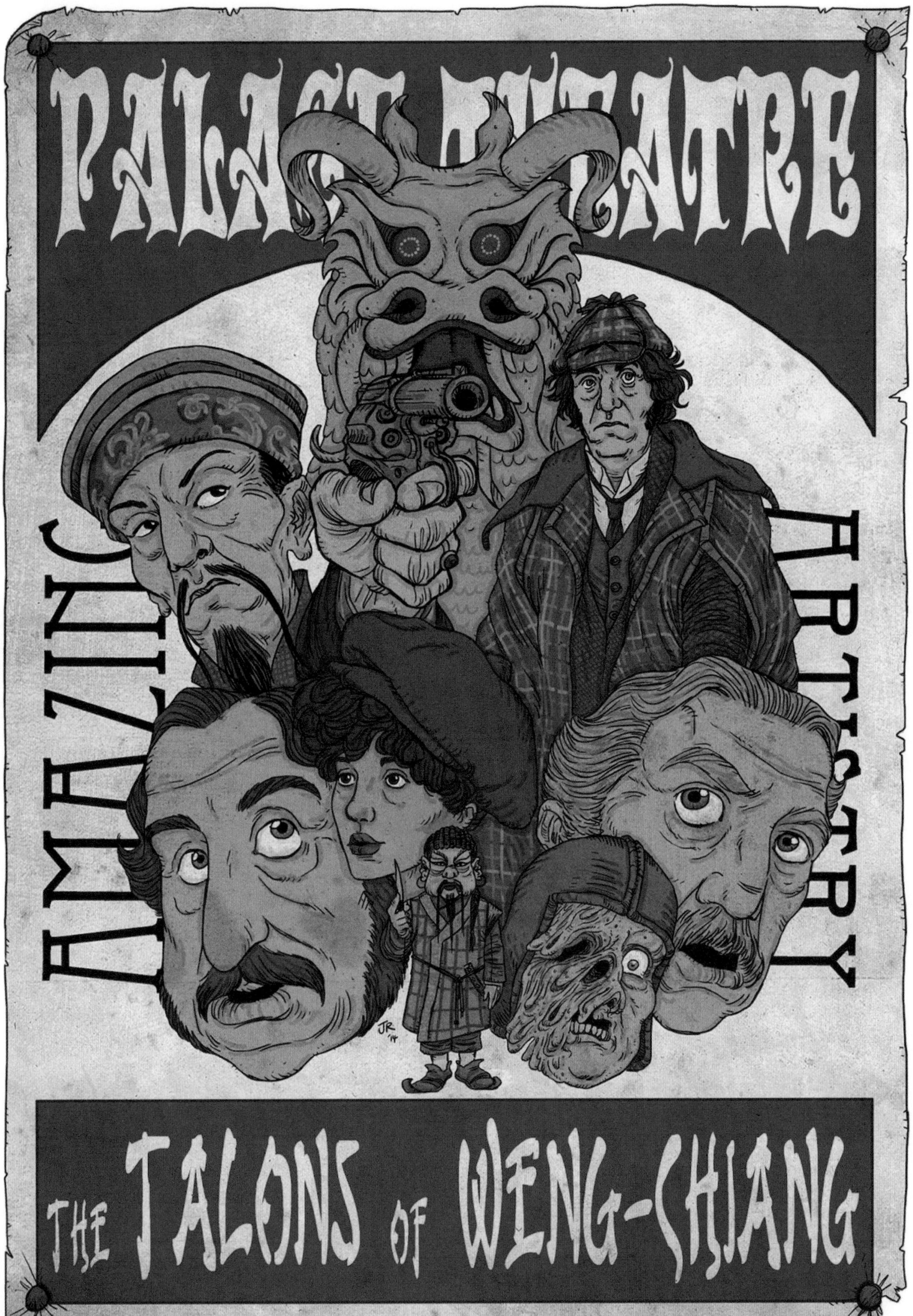
AMAZING
THE TALONS OF WENG-CHIANG

34
Horror of Fang Rock

An adventure for: Fourth Doctor and Leela
First shown: 3–24 September 1977 (4 episodes)
Written by: Terrance Dicks

The Doctor takes Leela to see Brighton, but arrives instead on Fang Rock in the early twentieth century. It is a foggy, inhospitable island with a lighthouse. Something is bleeding off the light's power, and one of the lighthouse keepers has disappeared.

Fang Rock is cut off from the mainland by a sudden fog, in which a ship is wrecked. The survivors gather in the lighthouse, but soon find themselves under siege by an alien killer.

The alien is a Rutan – a gelatinous green blob. The Rutans are the sworn enemies of the Sontarans, and just as ruthless. They hope to use Earth as a strategic base, and this Rutan is scouting out the possibilities and potential resistance. If the Doctor is to prevent an invasion, he has to destroy not just this Rutan, but also its mothership.

Using shape-shifting techniques to imitate members of the lighthouse crew, the Rutan kills everyone except the Doctor and Leela. Leela manages to destroy the Rutan, while the Doctor turns the lighthouse itself into a laser weapon to shoot down the mothership.

RIGHT: Illustration by Gareth Thomas

35

The Invasion of Time

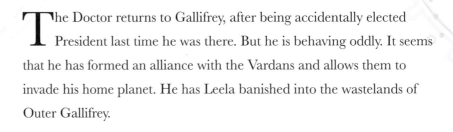

An adventure for:	Fourth Doctor, Leela and K-9
First shown:	4 February–11 March 1978 (6 episodes)
Written by:	David Agnew (Graham Williams and Anthony Read)

The Doctor returns to Gallifrey, after being accidentally elected President last time he was there. But he is behaving oddly. It seems that he has formed an alliance with the Vardans and allows them to invade his home planet. He has Leela banished into the wastelands of Outer Gallifrey.

The Vardans can travel along any waveform – even thought. The Doctor has banished Leela to keep her safe, and had the President's office lined with lead that will shield his thoughts. Now that he has forced the invaders to commit themselves, he can defeat them and, with K-9's help, time-loops their home planet.

But just as victory seems certain, a force of Sontarans arrive. They were using the Vardans to gain access to Gallifrey. They hunt the Doctor through the rooms and corridors of the TARDIS, but the Doctor is able to defeat them using a powerful weapon from Time Lord mythos – the Demat Gun.

Leela and K-9 decide to stay on Gallifrey as the Doctor leaves – but just as the TARDIS dematerialises, the Doctor reveals that he has already built himself another K-9: K-9 Mk 2!

RIGHT: Illustration by Alexandra Bowman

36
City of Death

An adventure for:	Fourth Doctor and Romana
First shown:	29 September–20 October 1979 (4 episodes)
Written by:	David Agnew (Douglas Adams, Graham Williams and David Fisher)

The Doctor and Romana visit Paris in 1979, where they experience strange time-shifts. The cause of these shifts is a man named Count Scarlioni, who is sponsoring time experiments carried out by the brilliant Professor Karensky.

Working with a British private detective called Duggan, the Doctor discovers that Scarlioni is planning to steal the Mona Lisa from the Louvre to finance his experiments. He has six more 'genuine' Mona Lisa paintings – all actually painted by the real Leonardo da Vinci – and plans to sell all seven.

The Doctor travels back to 1505 to see Leonardo and meets Captain Tancredi – another 'aspect' of Scarlioni. They are both aliases of an alien Jagaroth called Scaroth. When his spaceship exploded on prehistoric Earth, Scaroth was splintered through time. His various selves have been working to ensure that the furthest forward in time – Scarlioni – can travel back in time and save himself and his people from the explosion that killed them.

But that same explosion also kick-started the process of life on Earth, so the Doctor, Romana and Duggan have no choice but to stop him. Scaroth uses his own time equipment to travel back in time to try and stop the original explosion. The Doctor, Duggan and Romana follow him in the TARDIS. Duggan knocks Scarlioni out just in time and the spaceship explodes.

RIGHT: Illustration by Damian Street

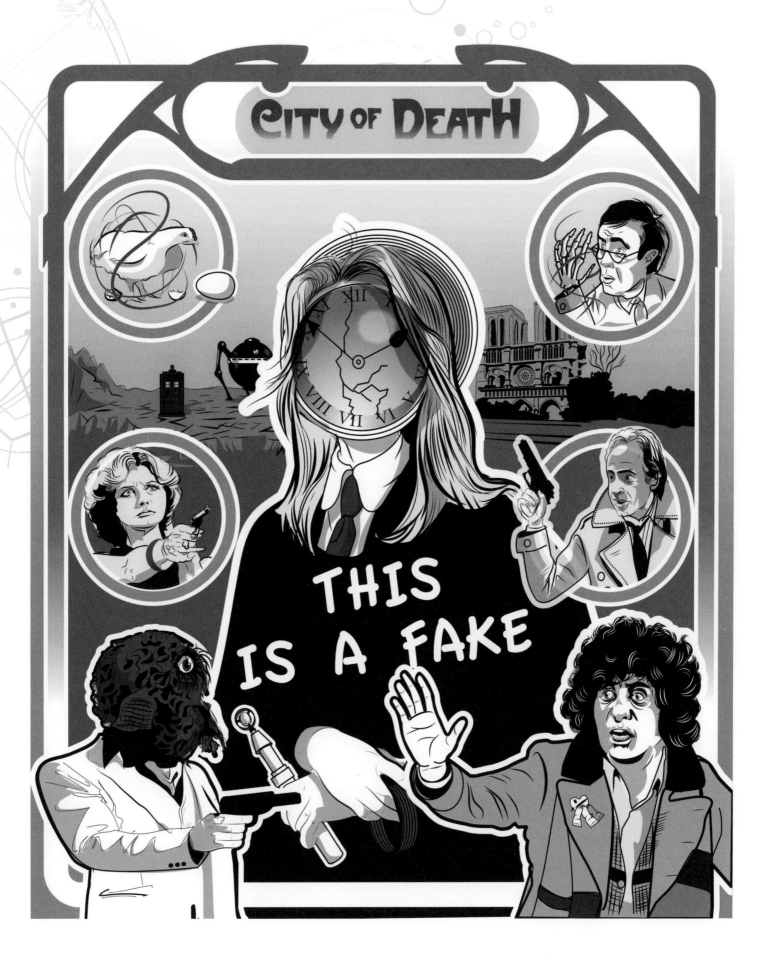

37
Logopolis

An adventure for: Fourth Doctor, Adric, Nyssa and Tegan
First shown: 28 February–21 March 1981 (4 episodes)
Written by: Christopher H Bidmead

Finally deciding to repair the TARDIS's chameleon circuit, the Doctor travels to England to find a real police box, but ends up falling into a trap set for him by the Master.

An Australian air hostess named Tegan Jovanka enters the TARDIS, believing it to be a real police box. Taking Tegan and Adric with him, the Doctor decides to seek the help of the Logopolitans, mathematical geniuses who live on the planet Logopolis. He hopes they will be able to reconfigure the exterior of the TARDIS. The mysterious Watcher transports Nyssa from Traken to join the other time travellers, warning the Doctor that a great ordeal lies ahead.

The Master also arrives on Logopolis and kills some of its inhabitants. Their leader, the Monitor, confesses to the renegade Time Lord that the Logopolitans are keeping the Universe in existence by beaming out complex calculations from a radio telescope, which is an exact copy of the Pharos Project radio telescope on Earth.

However, the Master has interrupted this process and the only way for the Doctor to save the Universe is to work with his nemesis. They beam a copy of the Logopolitans' program into space from the Earth's Pharos radio telescope, but the Master uses this as an opportunity to threaten the peoples of the entire Cosmos.

The two Time Lords fight, the Doctor falling from the radio telescope while the Master makes his escape. At this point, the Watcher reappears, fusing with the Doctor as he regenerates once more.

RIGHT: Illustration by Martyn Burdon

38 Castrovalva

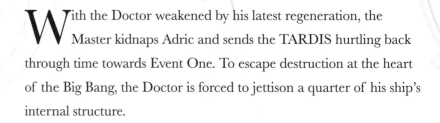

An adventure for:	Fifth Doctor, Adric, Nyssa and Tegan
First shown:	4–12 January 1982 (4 episodes)
Written by:	Christopher H Bidmead

With the Doctor weakened by his latest regeneration, the Master kidnaps Adric and sends the TARDIS hurtling back through time towards Event One. To escape destruction at the heart of the Big Bang, the Doctor is forced to jettison a quarter of his ship's internal structure.

Nyssa and Tegan then take the Doctor to the city of Castrovalva, on the planet Andromeda, hoping that he will be able to recover from the trauma of his regeneration there. However, Castrovalva is actually a dimensional paradox, a fictional construct created by the Master – with the aid of Adric's Block Transfer Computation calculations – for the sole purpose of destroying the Doctor. Even the inhabitants are part of the mathematical recursion affecting the city, while the Portreeve is actually the Master in disguise.

When all seems lost, one of the Castrovalvans, librarian Shardovan, sacrifices himself to free Adric, the Doctor having managed to make some of the city's fictional inhabitants self-aware. As the computation starts to collapse, the city folds in on itself and is destroyed. The Doctor and his companions escape, but so does the Master.

RIGHT: Illustration by Natasha Knight

39
Black Orchid

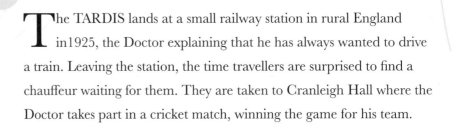

An adventure for:	Fifth Doctor, Adric, Nyssa and Tegan
First shown:	1–2 March 1982 (2 episodes)
Written by:	Terence Dudley

The TARDIS lands at a small railway station in rural England in1925, the Doctor explaining that he has always wanted to drive a train. Leaving the station, the time travellers are surprised to find a chauffeur waiting for them. They are taken to Cranleigh Hall where the Doctor takes part in a cricket match, winning the game for his team.

On the strength of his performance, Lord Charles Cranleigh invites them all to a fancy-dress party to be held that evening. Tegan is fascinated by a beautiful black orchid, which Lady Cranleigh, Charles's mother, says was found by her other son, George, who died on a botanical expedition to Brazil.

But George is not dead. He is being kept prisoner in the house, becoming unstable after the South American tribe that revere the black orchid disfigured him and cut out his tongue as a punishment for taking it.

George escapes his restraints and, desperate to be reunited with his fiancée, Ann, goes on a murderous rampage, the Doctor even being accused of his crimes at one point. George is finally cornered on the roof of Cranleigh Hall and falls to his death. Following his funeral, the TARDIS crew depart.

RIGHT: Illustration by Davey Beauchamp

40
Earthshock

An adventure for: Fifth Doctor, Adric, Nyssa and Tegan
First shown: 8–16 March 1982 (4 episodes)
Written by: Eric Saward

The TARDIS lands on Earth in the twenty-sixth century. A group of security troopers has been attacked by faceless androids in an underground cave system. The Doctor manages to help them destroy the androids, and finds they were guarding a huge bomb. Tracing the control signals for the bomb, the Doctor and his friends take the troopers to a space freighter where the signals originated from. The crew seem to know nothing about the bomb – but then hundreds of storage silos on board burst open to reveal Cybermen.

The Cybermen had planned to use the bomb to destroy an important conference where an alliance against them would be agreed. Now that the Doctor has disarmed the bomb, they decide to crash the freighter into the conference.

The freighter malfunctions and falls back through time. Instead of destroying the conference, the crash causes the extinction of the dinosaurs 65 million years ago. Sadly, the Doctor's companion Adric is also killed as he tries to prevent the crash.

RIGHT: Illustration by Nick Neocleous

41
The Five Doctors

An adventure for: First, Second, Third, Fourth, Fifth Doctors
                        and many companions
First shown: 25 November 1983
Written by: Terrance Dicks

The first five Doctors are taken out of time and space and transported – along with a selection of their companions – to the Death Zone on Gallifrey. Here, in ancient times, the Time Lords brought alien creatures to battle against each other in a series of games that were ended by Rassilon.

The Fourth Doctor is caught in the time vortex and never arrives. But the others find themselves battling against hostile alien creatures, including a Yeti, a Raston Warrior Robot, a Dalek, and a troop of Cybermen . . .

The Time Lords send the Master to help the Doctors – who of course do not trust him. Instead, the Master allies himself with the Cybermen, but later betrays them too.

Everyone converges on the Dark Tower – Rassilon's tomb in the heart of the Death Zone. It turns out that President Borusa has brought the Doctors here so that they can gain access to the tomb, as Borusa craves the gift of eternal life that Rassilon is said to hold.

But the tomb is itself a trap! The spirit of Rassilon appears, turns Borusa into stone and sends the first four Doctors back to their own time streams. The Time Lords want the Fifth Doctor to remain as President, which he cannot refuse. But the Doctor tricks them, leaving Councillor Flavia 'temporarily' in charge, and leaves in the TARDIS.

RIGHT: Illustration by Benjamin Gubb

42
Resurrection of the Daleks

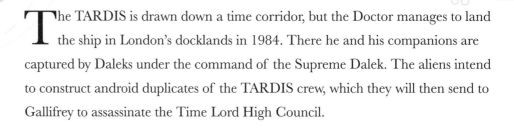

An adventure for: Fifth Doctor, Tegan and Turlough
First shown: 8–15 February 1984 (2 episodes)
Written by: Eric Saward

The TARDIS is drawn down a time corridor, but the Doctor manages to land the ship in London's docklands in 1984. There he and his companions are captured by Daleks under the command of the Supreme Dalek. The aliens intend to construct android duplicates of the TARDIS crew, which they will then send to Gallifrey to assassinate the Time Lord High Council.

In the far future, more Daleks attack a prison space station orbiting Earth, intending to free its only prisoner, Davros. The Movellans have developed an anti-Dalek virus and the Daleks need their creator to culture an antidote. Freed by Lytton (an alien mercenary in the Daleks' employ), Davros takes control of the minds of a number of Daleks, and vows to take his revenge upon the Doctor.

Another of the Daleks' duplicates, a genetically engineered human called Stien, turns against his creators. As Davros succumbs to the virus, Stien activates a self-destruct switch, destroying both the Supreme Dalek's forces and Davros's Daleks that are now involved in a merciless civil war.

Meanwhile, on Earth, the Doctor uses the anti-Dalek virus to eliminate the rest of the invading aliens. Lytton decides to remain in the twentieth century while Tegan, who has had enough of all the violence, leaves the TARDIS.

RIGHT: Illustration by Colin Fenwick

43
The Caves of Androzani

An adventure for:	Fifth Doctor and Peri
First shown:	8–16 March 1984 (4 episodes)
Written by:	Robert Holmes

The Doctor and Peri arrive on the planet Androzani Minor, where the life-extending spectrox drug, produced by bats, is mined in the planet's cave system. Production of the valuable spectrox is controlled by ruthless industrialist Morgus, but production is being disrupted by disfigured madman Sharaz Jek and his android rebels. The Doctor and Peri explore the caves and are captured by a General Chellak, leading government troops against Jek. The Doctor and Peri are sentenced to death but Jek 'rescues' them, craving intelligent and beautiful company.

Jek doesn't realise that both the Doctor and Peri have been infected by raw spectrox while exploring the caves. In its raw form it is highly toxic, and the Doctor and Peri are dying.

Jek's rebellion has closed down spectrox mining. Morgus is desperate to get it started again, and there is a battle between the army, mercenaries working for Morgus and Jek's androids. Jek and Morgus are both killed. The Doctor manages to find the antidote to the toxic spectrox – the milk of a queen bat – and gives it to Peri.

But there isn't enough of the antidote for the Doctor as well, and he collapses in the TARDIS – regenerating into his sixth form . . .

ABOVE: Illustration by Tori Henry

ABOVE: Illustration by Andrew Kennedy

44
The Twin Dilemma

An adventure for:	Sixth Doctor and Peri
First shown:	22–30 March 1984 (4 episodes)
Written by:	Anthony Steven

Following the events of *The Caves of Androzani*, the Doctor's latest regeneration causes him to behave erratically, even going so far as to attack Peri, thinking she is a spy.

Meanwhile a pair of mathematical genius twins, Romulus and Remus Sylvest, are abducted from Earth by the mysterious Professor Edgeworth and transported to a craft positioned in deep space. From there he takes them to the asteroid Titan III, under the instruction of a slug-like alien called Mestor, the Tyrant of Jaconda. Mestor intends to plunge the planet Jaconda, which his Gastropod race has taken over, into its own sun so that the resulting explosion might spread Gastropod eggs across the Cosmos. Mestor needs the twins' equation-solving skills to make this happen.

Despite intending to become a hermit in remorse for attacking Peri, the Doctor ends up involved in Edgeworth's schemes. Edgeworth is revealed to be the renegade Time Lord Azmael. Peri is captured by the Jacondans and brought before Mestor. When he realises the danger she's in, the Doctor finally demonstrates compassion towards her.

Ultimately, the two Time Lords foil Mestor's plans, along with the help of Lieutenant Hugo Lang of the Intergalactic Task Force. After Mestor possesses Azmael's body, Azmael commits suicide by means of a final fatal regeneration, destroying the tyrant's mind in the process.

RIGHT: Illustration by Finn Clark

45
The Mark of the Rani

An adventure for: Sixth Doctor and Peri
First shown: 2–9 February 1985 (2 episodes)
Written by: Pip and Jane Baker

In the mining village of Killingworth, in early nineteenth-century England, miners are being turned into Luddites, who then set about attacking both men and machinery.

The TARDIS lands in the village when the Doctor decides to investigate a time distortion. The Doctor and Peri meet Lord Ravensworth, the local landowner, who is disturbed by the attacks, telling them that the most passive of men are suddenly turning violent, and that somehow the local bathhouse is involved.

At the same time, the Master arrives, intending to accelerate the Industrial Revolution for his own nefarious ends. However, he is not counting on the Rani, a renegade Time Lord, being there. Disguised as the old lady who runs the bathhouse, she has been stealing the neuro-chemicals that induce sleep from the miners. The Master and the Rani form an uneasy alliance in order to deal with the Doctor, convincing the locals to push the TARDIS down a mine shaft.

The Doctor is saved from death by the inventor George Stephenson, and ends up turning the tables on the renegades. The Master and the Rani escape in her TARDIS, along with a Tyrannosaurus rex embryo the Rani had collected on another trip to Earth. But the Doctor has sabotaged her TARDIS, which spins uncontrollably towards the edge of the Universe – while on board, the T. rex embryo begins to grow . . .

The Doctor restores the local population to normal before departing – his own TARDIS having been retrieved from the mine by Ravensworth.

RIGHT: Illustration by Ian Leaver

46

Revelation of the Daleks

An adventure for:	Sixth Doctor and Peri
First shown:	23–30 March 1985 (2 episodes)
Written by:	Eric Saward

The Doctor and Peri visit the planet Necros, where the Doctor has heard his old friend Stengos has died, and is resting in a cemetery called Tranquil Repose. In fact, the facility cryogenically freezes people until a cure can be found for their condition. Or so everyone thinks.

The Great Healer in charge of the complex is actually Davros, who is turning suitable people – including Stengos – into a new race of Daleks. Those who are not suitable he is 'recycling' as food for the starving millions of the galaxy. Davros's business partner, Kara, plans to double-cross him and sends an assassin called Orcini to kill him.

Takis, another worker at Tranquil Repose, also betrays Davros – to the Supreme Dalek on Skaro who sends a task force to take Davros prisoner. The Doctor and Orcini use a powerful bomb to destroy Davros's new army of Daleks, just as the Daleks of Skaro leave with Davros as their prisoner . . .

RIGHT: Illustration by Mark Price

REVELATION OF THE DALEKS

47
The Trial of a Time Lord

An adventure for:	Sixth Doctor, Peri and Mel
First shown:	6 September–6 December 1986 (14 episodes)
Written by:	Robert Holmes, Philip Martin, Pip and Jane Baker, and Eric Saward

The TARDIS is forcibly drawn to a vast space station where the Doctor faces a tribunal of Time Lords, accused of the crime of cosmic interference. The Doctor's memory of recent events is gone.

The Valeyard, acting as prosecutor, uses evidence taken from the Matrix as well as the TARDIS. He highlights events on Ravolox, a planet that turns out to be Earth two million years in the future and moved to a different location in space, as well as those on Thoros-Beta, home of the reptilian Mentors and their mind-controlled humanoid slaves.

The Doctor believes the evidence has been tampered with. In his defence, he presents an incident from his near future (after he has started travelling with a new companion, Melanie Bush), involving a murderous rampage by the vegetal Vervoids on the spaceliner Hyperion III. Following this recount, the Valeyard accuses the Doctor of genocide.

When it is revealed that the trial is, indeed, a set-up, intended to hide the actions of the High Council, the Valeyard (an amalgamation of the darker side of the Doctor between his twelfth and final regenerations) flees into the Matrix, but is pursued by the vindicated Time Lord.

With the High Council deposed, the Master tries to take over, but becomes trapped in the Matrix. The Doctor defeats the Valeyard and the charges against him are dismissed. He then sets off on his travels again, now accompanied by Mel.

RIGHT: Illustration by Chris Sick

ABOVE: Illustration by Karen Kalbacher

48
Paradise Towers

An adventure for:	Seventh Doctor and Mel
First shown:	5–26 October 1987 (4 episodes)
Written by:	Stephen Wyatt

The Doctor and Mel arrive at Paradise Towers – a luxury residential building – but are shocked to find the place derelict and now home only to rats, the teenage Kangs, the older Rezzies, and the Caretakers. The Kangs are identified by colour, with rival colour factions engaging in deadly gang warfare.

The Doctor is mistaken for the Great Architect by the Caretakers, while Mel has tea with the cannibalistic Tilda and Tabby, before she meets Pex – a vigilante who turns out to have hidden to avoid fighting in the war, which is where the rest of the population went.

The Doctor escapes the Caretakers and ends up at the Red Kangs' 'brainquarters' where he tries to find out more about the mechanical-claw-creature depicted in their graffiti-like 'wallscrawls'.

Mel and Pex are captured by the Blue Kangs. Mel is allowed to go but ends up as Tilda and Tabby's prisoner – who have no intention of letting her leave this time – until they are killed by the robotic Cleaners.

The Doctor is brought before the Chief Caretaker and learns that Kroagnon, the Great Architect, disappeared after the completion of Paradise Towers. Kroagnon is actually the creature lurking in the basement. Transplanting his brain into the Chief Caretaker's body, he plans to destroy everyone in the Towers, until Pex sacrifices himself, blowing them both up.

ABOVE: Illustration by Freya Verrall

49
Dragonfire

An adventure for:	Seventh Doctor, Mel and Ace
First shown:	23 November–7 December 1987 (3 episodes)
Written by:	Ian Briggs

At the trading colony of Iceworld, on the planet Svartos, the Doctor and Mel meet an old acquaintance, the mercenary Sabalom Glitz. Glitz owes money to Kane, the megalomaniac ruler of Iceworld, and will lose his ship if he doesn't settle his debt. Searching for a treasure guarded by a dragon in the frozen caverns beyond Iceworld, Glitz doesn't realise he is being used by Kane who wants the treasure for himself.

While the Doctor and Glitz go treasure-hunting, Mel meets Ace, a girl from late twentieth-century Earth who arrived on Iceworld after a chemistry experiment went wrong. Following a security incident, they are arrested and interrogated by Kane, who tries to tempt Ace to become one of his mercenaries, but they escape.

In the ice caverns the Doctor and Glitz meet the dragon, a bipedal mechanoid, as well as Mel

and Ace. The dragon shows them a hologram that explains that Kane is an alien criminal and Iceworld is a huge spacecraft and effectively Kane's prison. The crystal Kane seeks is the key to controlling the spacecraft and is hidden inside the dragon's head.

Eventually, Kane's troops destroy the dragon and remove its head, which the Doctor then acquires. Meanwhile, Kane has captured Ace, so the Doctor agrees to give Kane the crystal in exchange for her life. Kane sets a course for his home planet to take revenge on his people, but discovers it no longer exists. Devastated, he kills himself by exposing himself to light rays, which melt him.

Glitz claims Iceworld for his own and Mel decides to stay with him, while Ace joins the Doctor in the TARDIS.

RIGHT: Illustration by
Jessica Baynes

50
Remembrance of the Daleks

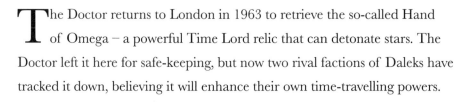

An adventure for: Seventh Doctor and Ace
First shown: 5–26 October 1988 (4 episodes)
Written by: Ben Aaronovitch

The Doctor returns to London in 1963 to retrieve the so-called Hand of Omega – a powerful Time Lord relic that can detonate stars. The Doctor left it here for safe-keeping, but now two rival factions of Daleks have tracked it down, believing it will enhance their own time-travelling powers.

Led by the Supreme Dalek, the Rebel Dalek faction has allied itself with a group of fascists, and managed to track down the Hand of Omega to a graveyard. But the Imperial Daleks – loyal to the Emperor Dalek – arrive to do battle with the rival Dalek faction. They bring with them a powerful Special Weapons Dalek that destroys the renegade Dalek patrols.

The Doctor does his best to stop the military, led by Group Captain Gilmore, from getting caught in the middle of the battle. In fact, the Doctor has set a clever trap, and wants the Daleks to get the Hand of Omega. The Emperor Dalek – who turns out to be Davros – believes he is victorious. But the Doctor has programmed the Hand of Omega to destroy the Dalek planet Skaro with a gigantic supernova. It also destroys the Dalek Imperial mothership, but not before Davros flees in an escape pod . . .

RIGHT: Illustration by David North

51
Battlefield

An adventure for:	Seventh Doctor, Ace and the Brigadier
First shown:	6–27 September 1989 (4 episodes)
Written by:	Ben Aaronovitch

The TARDIS materialises in the English countryside near the village of Carbury. Nearby, a nuclear missile convoy, under the command of UNIT Brigadier Winifred Bambera, has run into difficulties. Lying on the bed of nearby Lake Vortigern is a spaceship from another dimension containing the body of King Arthur, supposedly held in suspended animation, along with his sword, Excalibur.

Ancelyn, a knight from the same dimension as the spaceship, arrives on Earth to aid Arthur, but is followed by his rival Mordred and the sorceress Morgaine. They all recognise the Doctor, believing him to be Merlin, which the Time Lord puts down to events that have yet to occur in his own future.

A battle breaks out between UNIT and Morgaine's army. Brigadier Lethbridge-Stewart comes out of retirement to deal with the crisis, using silver bullets to kill the Destroyer – a powerful creature unleashed by Morgaine so that it might devour the world – although he almost dies in the process.

Morgaine tries to fire the nuclear missile, but is dissuaded when the Doctor reveals to her what nuclear war would really mean, and that Arthur is in fact dead. Defeated, Morgaine and Mordred are taken prisoner by UNIT.

RIGHT: Illustration by Francis McHardy

52
The Curse of Fenric

An adventure for:	Seventh Doctor and Ace
First shown:	25 October–15 November 1989 (4 episodes)
Written by:	Ian Briggs

The Doctor and Ace arrive at a secret military base during World War II, where scientist Judson has invented the Ultima Machine to decrypt German ciphers. The base commander, Millington, has located a source of deadly poison below the church and plans to use this against the enemy. As Russian troops arrive to try to steal the Ultima Machine, the Doctor deduces from local Viking legends that Fenric, an ancient evil from the dawn of time, is about to be released.

The Doctor defeated Fenric centuries ago using an unsolvable chess problem, and imprisoned him in a flask – but now Fenric is returning and has sent his 'wolves', who include Judson, Millington and Ace, to prepare for his arrival. With vampiric Haemovores called up by Fenric emerging from the sea, the Doctor and Ace battle to prevent Fenric's return, but to no avail!

The Doctor once again sets Fenric a chess problem, and persuades the Ancient One – a powerful Haemovore brought back from the future – to turn against Fenric. The Ancient One kills Fenric and sacrifices himself in the process.

RIGHT: Illustration by Jake Summer

53
Survival

An adventure for: Seventh Doctor and Ace

First shown: 22 November–6 December 1989 (3 episodes)

Written by: Rona Munro

The Doctor and Ace return to her home in Perivale, where they discover a mysterious black cat roaming the streets and humans – notably Ace's old friends – being hunted and taken to another world.

When another young man is abducted, Ace follows, hunted by a Cheetah Person on horseback. The Doctor, along with a keep-fit instructor called Paterson, is teleported to the planet of the Cheetah People, where he finds his old nemesis, the Master, waiting for him.

The Master is slowly transforming into a Cheetah Person and is using the black cat – a kitling – to create a dimensional bridge, so that the Cheetah People – who once had a great civilisation before they regressed into animals – can hunt prey on Earth. The planet itself is alive, but also dying, and clearly dangerous.

Ace's friend Midge succumbs to the power of the planet and turns into a beast. The Master uses Midge to teleport back to Earth and escape the dying world. Ace is also turning into a Cheetah Person and the Doctor uses her to help the rest of them return to Perivale.

The Master takes the Doctor back to the planet of the Cheetah People for one final confrontation before the Doctor teleports back to Earth, leaving his nemesis trapped on the dying world.

RIGHT: Illustration by Karen Kalbacher

54
Doctor Who: The Movie

An adventure for:	Seventh Doctor, Eighth Doctor and Grace
First shown:	14 May 1996
Written by:	Matthew Jacobs

The Master is executed by the Daleks on Skaro and the Doctor is charged with returning his physical remains to Gallifrey. However, the Master turns into a snake-like creature and slithers into the TARDIS console, causing it to land in San Francisco on the eve of the new millennium.

Emerging from the TARDIS, the Doctor is shot by a gang and appears to die whilst being operated on by Dr Grace Holloway. However, being shot has actually caused his body to regenerate.

Also having left the TARDIS, the Master takes over the body of an ambulance driver and puts into action a plan to use the TARDIS's power source – the Eye of Harmony – to destroy the Earth.

Convincing Grace that he is the same man she operated on, the newly regenerated Doctor persuades her to help him. They are also joined by Chang Lee, a reformed gang member, and eventually manage to foil the Master's plan, the Master himself being sucked into the Eye of Harmony.

The Doctor invites Grace to travel with him in the TARDIS, but she refuses, and so the Time Lord sets off again on his travels through time and space, alone.

ABOVE: Illustration by Kendra Sterken

ABOVE: Illustration by Gwyneth Gillett

55
Rose

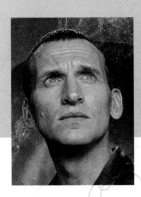

An adventure for:	Ninth Doctor and Rose
First shown:	26 March 2005
Written by:	Russell T Davies

Rose Tyler works in a London department store. After the shop closes one night, she is attacked in the basement by plastic mannequins. They are Autons controlled by the Nestene Consciousness. A stranger rescues her, introducing himself as the Doctor. Later he turns up at Rose and her mum's flat, where he is attacked by a plastic arm detached from an Auton.

The Doctor leaves hurriedly and Rose and Mickey, Rose's boyfriend, try to track him down. During the process Mickey is replaced with a plastic Nestene duplicate, which also wants to hunt down the Doctor. The Doctor turns up again to rescue Rose – who is amazed when she enters the TARDIS to find it bigger on the inside . . .

Together the Doctor and Rose track down the Nestene Consciousness and rescue Mickey. As Auton display dummies come to life all over Britain and smash their way out of shop windows, the Doctor and Rose manage to destroy the Nestene Consciousness with anti-plastic.

And despite Mickey's advice, once the adventure is over, Rose is unable to resist the chance to travel with the Doctor in the TARDIS again . . .

RIGHT: Illustration by Callum Holland

56
Dalek

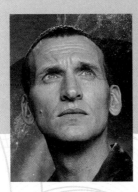

An adventure for:	Ninth Doctor and Rose
First shown:	30 April 2005
Written by:	Robert Shearman

Rich and powerful, Henry Van Statten collects alien artefacts and stores them in a huge complex hidden deep beneath the Utah desert. One of the artefacts he has bought is an alien creature housed inside an armoured shell. Despite the efforts of Van Statten's team, the imprisoned creature won't communicate with them.

Then the Doctor and Rose arrive – and the Doctor recognises the creature as a Dalek. The Dalek also recognises the Doctor. Absorbing energy from Rose, who has travelled in time, the Dalek returns to full strength and breaks free of its chains. It escapes from its cell and sets about exterminating all humans – starting with Van Statten's security troops.

But the Dalek has been affected by the energy it absorbed from Rose, influenced by her human DNA. This alters its reasoning and outlook, and rather than live with the shame of not being a 'pure' Dalek, the creature destroys itself.

RIGHT: Illustration by Kat Lunoe

57
Father's Day

An adventure for:	Ninth Doctor and Rose
First shown:	14 May 2005
Written by:	Paul Cornell

The Doctor reluctantly agrees to take Rose back to 1987, to the day when her father, Pete Tyler, was killed in a hit-and-run accident. Despite the Doctor's warnings, Rose is unable to stand by and watch – and rushes out to save her father's life. The Doctor's anger turns to concern as Reapers detect the changed history and start to attack. The Reapers are creatures from outside time that take advantage of points in time and space where time itself has been damaged in some way. They are drawn to the 'wound' like bacteria. But unlike bacteria they sterilise the wound – by destroying everything inside it.

Under siege by the Reapers in the local church along with a wedding party, the Doctor hopes to use the TARDIS to heal the wound and restore normality – and with Rose's dad surviving, too.

But a Reaper breaks into the church. It consumes the Doctor and breaks the link with the TARDIS. Pete sacrifices himself to put history back on track. He throws himself under the car that originally killed him, restoring the Doctor and the other victims of the Reapers.

ABOVE: Illustration by Liz Driver

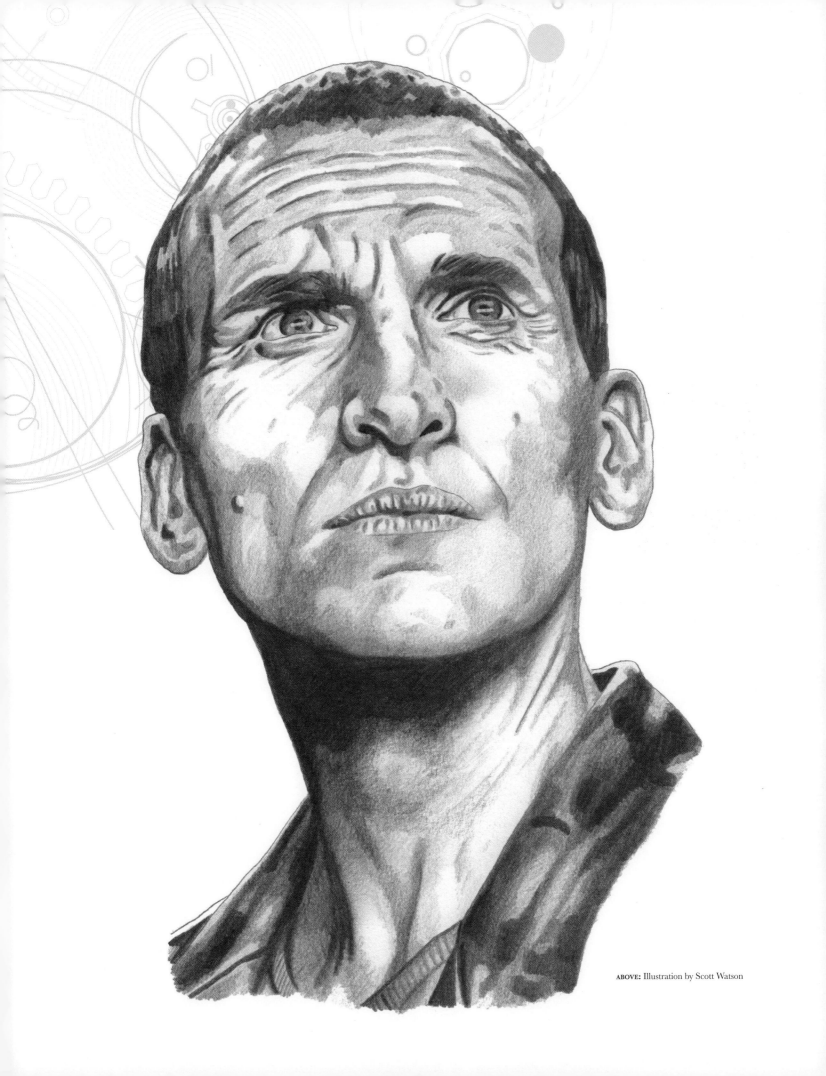

ABOVE: Illustration by Scott Watson

58

The Empty Child/
The Doctor Dances

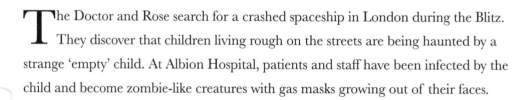

An adventure for:	Ninth Doctor, Rose and Captain Jack
First shown:	21–28 May 2005 (2 episodes)
Written by:	Steven Moffat

The Doctor and Rose search for a crashed spaceship in London during the Blitz. They discover that children living rough on the streets are being haunted by a strange 'empty' child. At Albion Hospital, patients and staff have been infected by the child and become zombie-like creatures with gas masks growing out of their faces.

Meeting the mysterious ex-Time Agent Captain Jack Harkness, the Doctor and Rose discover that the crashed ship was a Chula medical ship. The interior was filled with nanogenes, which leaked out after the crash. These nanogenes used the first human they found as a template from which to 'repair' all other humans. That human was the child, Jamie, who had almost been killed in an earlier air raid. Now the nanogenes are about to remodel the entire human race on a terrified child wearing a gas mask and searching for his mother – also equipped with superhuman strength, to fight as a Chula Warrior.

When Jamie is reunited with his mother, the nanogenes realise her DNA must carry the correct genetic information for humans, and the damage is corrected. The Doctor destroys the crashed spaceship and saves Jack from a bomb, taking him on board the TARDIS.

RIGHT: Illustration by Melanie Miller

59

Bad Wolf/
The Parting of the Ways

An adventure for:	Ninth Doctor, Rose and Captain Jack
First shown:	11–18 June 2005 (2 episodes)
Written by:	Russell T Davies

The Doctor, Rose and Jack find themselves teleported aboard the Game Station where they are forced to take part in deadly TV game shows. The Doctor and Jack escape, but Rose is apparently killed. In fact she has again been teleported – to a Dalek spaceship.

For centuries, the Daleks have been manipulating humanity through broadcasts from the Game Station, run by the Bad Wolf Corporation. A lone Dalek ship survived the Great Time War against the Time Lords, and they have been building a new Dalek race using humans harvested from the games.

The Doctor and Jack rescue Rose from the Dalek flagship – where the Dalek Emperor

believes himself to be the god of all Daleks. He orders the purification of Earth by fire.

The Doctor sends Rose back to her own time as he and Jack organise resistance on the Game Station. Jack is killed and the Daleks capture the Doctor. But Rose realises that 'Bad Wolf', which she has seen and heard repeatedly, is a clue and that she can get back to the Doctor in the TARDIS.

During the process, Rose absorbs time-vortex energy from the TARDIS, which enables her to destroy the Daleks and bring Jack back to life – but at the cost of her own life. The Doctor saves her by absorbing the vortex energy, and regenerates into a new body . . .

RIGHT: Illustration by
Adina Kinac

60

The Christmas Invasion

An adventure for:	Tenth Doctor and Rose
First shown:	25 December 2005
Written by:	Russell T Davies

On Christmas Eve 2005, the TARDIS crashes on the Powell Estate in London. A strange man stumbles out, wishing Jackie Tyler and Mickey Smith a Merry Christmas before collapsing. Rose emerges after him and explains that the stranger is the Doctor. They take him to Jackie's flat, dress him in pyjamas, and put him to bed. Meanwhile, a space probe destined for Mars is swallowed by a massive spaceship which looks like a floating island.

While out Christmas shopping, Rose and Mickey are attacked by robot Santas. Back at Jackie's flat, a Christmas tree also tries to kill them, until the Doctor stops it with his sonic screwdriver. Before losing consciousness again, he tells them that something bigger is coming.

The first image sent by the Mars probe is the face of the leader of the war-like alien race, the Sycorax.

Prime Minister Harriet Jones and UNIT monitor the situation from inside the Tower of London. The Sycorax demand the planet's surrender, but the PM declines, so as a threat, the aliens induce anyone with the blood type A+ to prepare to jump off the top of the nearest building.

The Sycorax ship enters the Earth's atmosphere. The TARDIS – with the Doctor, Rose, Jackie and Mickey on board – is transmatted aboard. A revived Doctor emerges and frees the blood-controlled humans before finally fighting the Sycorax leader for control of the planet. He wins, but only after losing a hand, which promptly regrows as he is still in the first fifteen hours of his regeneration cycle.

The Doctor sends the Sycorax packing, but as their ship leaves Earth, Harriet Jones orders Torchwood to destroy it, provoking the Doctor's ire.

ABOVE: Illustration by Barbara Mary Temple

61
School Reunion

An adventure for:	Tenth Doctor, Rose, Mickey, Sarah and K-9
First shown:	29 April 2006
Written by:	Toby Whithouse

The Doctor and Rose go undercover at Deffry Vale High School. The Doctor becomes a supply teacher while Rose works as a dinner lady. Mickey has called them in to investigate how the school's results have improved so dramatically with the arrival of a new head teacher.

Sarah Jane Smith is also investigating the school, and along with K-9 the team discover that the head teacher and many of the staff are actually Krillitanes. They are cooking chips in Krillitane oil to enhance the abilities of the pupils, and using the brightest children to solve the so-called Skasis Paradigm. With this, Krillitanes will be able to control the very building blocks of time and space.

But the oil is also deadly to Krillitanes, and K-9 sacrifices himself to set fire to the oil and destroy the aliens. The Doctor again bids a sad farewell to Sarah. But he leaves her with a present – a completely repaired K-9.

RIGHT: Illustration by Vanessa Knott

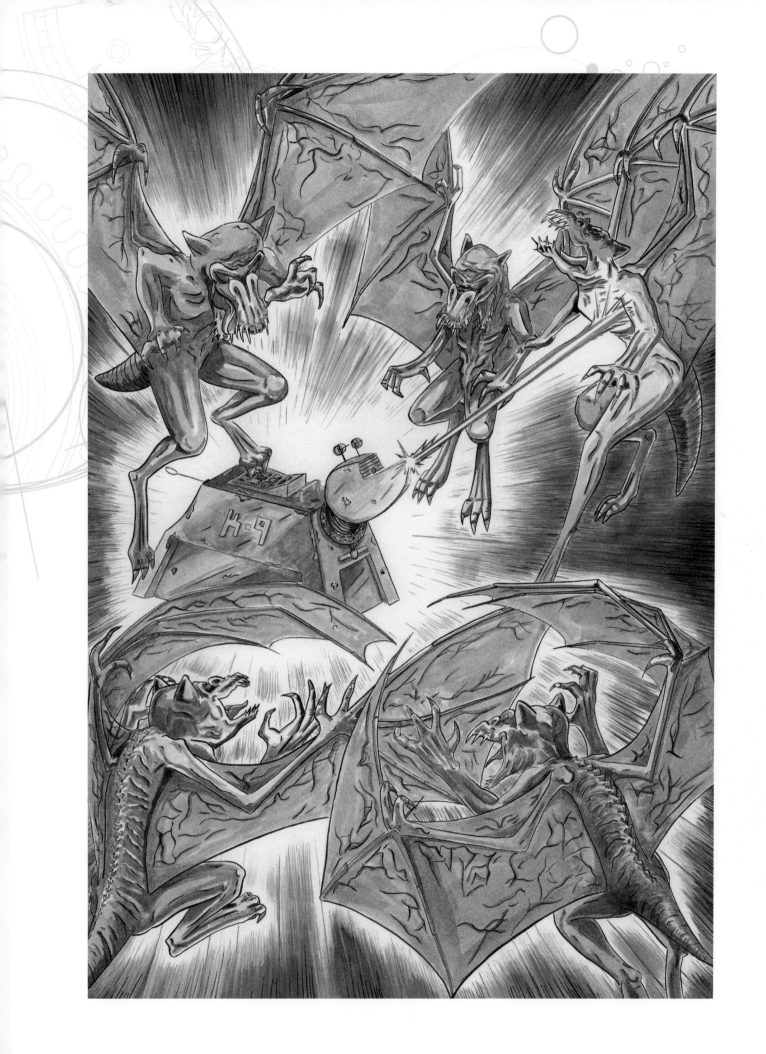

62
The Girl in the Fireplace

An adventure for:	Tenth Doctor, Rose and Mickey
First shown:	2 May 2006
Written by:	Steven Moffat

The Doctor and his friends arrive on board a drifting spaceship, which is damaged, but has been repaired by clockwork androids. The Doctor discovers a fireplace that links the ship with eighteenth-century France. There are several similar 'time windows' on the ship – all of them connected to points in the life of Madame de Pompadour, nicknamed Reinette.

The Doctor meets Reinette several times during her life, and realises that the repair androids have targeted her for some reason. They have used 'component parts' from the human crew to repair the ship, but still need a replacement 'brain' for the central computer. They believe that they can use Reinette's head to fulfil this need.

The Doctor manages to save Reinette from the androids, and promises to take her away with him. But when he returns for her through the time window, too much time has passed and he discovers Reinette has died, tragically young. The TARDIS leaves – the Doctor never realising that the spaceship's name is SS *Mme de Pompadour*, which is why the androids thought her brain could replace the central computer.

ABOVE: Illustration by Nathan Owens

RIGHT: Illustration by Judy Borror

63
The Impossible Planet/ The Satan Pit

An adventure for:	Tenth Doctor, Rose and Mickey
First shown:	3–10 June 2006 (2 episodes)
Written by:	Matt Jones

Sanctuary Base 6 is a research centre on a planet in an impossible orbit around a black hole. The human crew and their servants, the Ood, are drilling in search of the power source that keeps the planet from being sucked into the black hole.

But in fact, the planet is the ancient prison of the Beast, and if he wakes, the power that keeps the planet safe will cease and both prison and captive will be destroyed in the black hole. The Doctor and Rose arrive as the Beast awakens and begins to assert his influence over Ood and humans alike. An earth tremor plunges part of the base where the TARDIS has landed into an abyss. The Beast takes over the telepathic Ood, turning them against the humans. It also possesses archaeologist Toby Zed. The Beast's plan is to hide inside Toby's body and escape with him and the other humans as they leave Sanctuary Base.

The Doctor finds the demonic form of the Beast chained up deep under the planet. Realising the truth, he plunges the planet into the black hole. Rose and the remaining crew hurry to the base's escape ship. Rose realises Toby is still possessed and pushes him out of the ship and into space. Meanwhile, the Doctor finds the TARDIS in the collapsing planet and uses its power to drag the escape ship away from the black hole to safety.

RIGHT: Illustration by Janet Nguyen

64
Army of Ghosts/Doomsday

An adventure for: Tenth Doctor and Rose
First shown: 1–8 July 2006 (2 episodes)
Written by: Russell T Davies

Returning to the Powell Estate, the Doctor and Rose discover that the human race is being visited by the ghosts of their dearly departed. Tracing one of the ghosts to its source, the Doctor learns that the spectral visitations coincide with the Torchwood Institute's attempts to extract energy from a breach between dimensions at the top of their Canary Wharf tower.

Torchwood needs the Doctor's help to identify a large sphere located in the building's basement. It is a void ship, and its arrival created the breach. The ghosts turn out to be Cybermen, now on Earth having travelled from Pete's World via dimensional cracks caused by Torchwood exploiting the breach. The cyborgs are pursued by Mickey Smith and his friends. The void ship opens, releasing its passengers:

four Daleks that form the Cult of Skaro! After the Cybermen fail to negotiate an alliance with the Daleks, the two races engage in battle.

The Doctor is transported to the parallel version of Earth but returns with Pete Tyler, just in time to save Rose from the Cult of Skaro. The aliens nonetheless manage to open the Genesis Ark they brought with them through the Void, releasing millions of imprisoned Daleks from inside.

Ultimately the Doctor fully opens the breach, sucking anything that has travelled through the Void back into it, including all of the Daleks and Cybermen – and very nearly dragging in Rose as well. She is saved by Pete at the last second and teleported to his world, but is cut off from the Doctor's universe forever . . .

RIGHT: Illustration by Stuart Manning

65
Human Nature/
The Family of Blood

An adventure for:	Tenth Doctor and Martha
First shown:	26 May–2 June 2007 (2 episodes)
Written by:	Paul Cornell

A group of predatory aliens called the Family of Blood tracks the Doctor to Earth in 1913. They are after the Doctor's immortal Time Lord 'essence' so that they can extend their short lives and live forever.

But the Doctor is in hiding. Using Chameleon Arch technology, his Time Lord nature and his memories are concealed inside a pocket watch and he has become a human called John Smith, teaching history at Farringham School. Only Martha, disguised as a maid at the school, knows the truth.

But the Family eventually find the Doctor. They possess several humans and animate scarecrows as their troops, eventually attacking the school. John Smith – who has no idea that he doesn't really exist – has fallen in love with the school matron, Joan Redfern. He has to choose between love, or sacrificing everything he believes to be true to save himself and his friends. Finally persuaded of the truth by Martha and Joan, he tricks the Family into thinking he is still Smith and will give them the essence, but in fact, he has already transformed back into the Doctor. He destroys their ship and metes out appropriate punishments to each of them. He asks Joan to travel with him, but she refuses.

RIGHT: Illustration by George Poland

66
Blink

An adventure for: Tenth Doctor and Martha
First shown: 9 June 2007
Written by: Steven Moffat

Taking photographs in an old, deserted house, Sally Sparrow finds a warning from the Doctor written underneath the old wallpaper. The Doctor and Martha are trapped in the 1960s – sent back there without the TARDIS by the touch of a Weeping Angel, a member of an alien race also known as the Lonely Assassins, who absorb the energy from people's unfulfilled lives when they send them back in time.

ABOVE: Illustration by Sadie Tovey

RIGHT: Illustration by Calee Rigdon

The Doctor has left other clues for Sally and her friend's brother Larry Nightingale, including 'Easter Egg' messages on her DVDs. Following these clues, Sally and Larry evade the Weeping Angels and find the TARDIS. They manage to send it back in time to rescue the Doctor and Martha, and the Weeping Angels are trapped – frozen to stone as they stand looking at each other.

67
Utopia/The Sound of Drums/ Last of the Time Lords

An adventure for: Tenth Doctor, Martha and Captain Jack
First shown: 16-30 June 2007 (3 episodes)
Written by: Russell T Davies

The Doctor, Martha and Jack arrive at the end of the Universe on the planet Malcassairo, and find a small group of human survivors has built a rocket to take them to 'Utopia'. The project is led by the brilliant Professor Yana, but Yana is in fact the Master – his personality hidden in an effort to escape the Time War. The Doctor's arrival awakens his old memories and personality, and the Master kills his companion Chantho. Injured, he regenerates into a younger form, and steals the Doctor's TARDIS.

The Doctor, Martha and Jack manage to get back to Earth, to discover that new Prime Minister, Harold Saxon, is in fact the Master – who returned years earlier. 'Saxon' assassinates his cabinet, and then claims to have made contact with benevolent aliens and sets up a meeting with the 'Toclafane'. But it's a trap. The Toclafane kill the US president, then billions of them appear to take over Earth.

For a year, the Master rules with the Toclafane – which are actually the future survivors of humanity – building a fleet of rockets to conquer other worlds.

As the Master holds the Doctor and his friends prisoner, it is up to Martha to organise the people of Earth against him. Twelve months on, she is captured, the weapon she's been building destroyed. But as the Master prepares to unleash the Toclafane on the Universe, Martha and the Doctor's real plan unfolds. Martha has told people across the world to concentrate their thoughts onto the Doctor at the same moment. This collective psychic energy routed through the Master's Archangel Network rejuvenates the Doctor. He reverts events to a year previously, before the appearance of the Toclafane. Betrayed, the Master's wife shoots him, and the Master dies in the Doctor's arms – refusing to regenerate, so the Doctor is left as the last Time Lord.

RIGHT: Illustration by Kylie Cowley

68
Voyage of the Damned

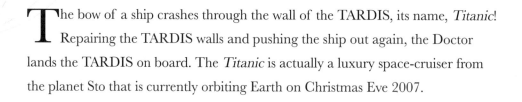

An adventure for: Tenth Doctor and Astrid
First shown: 25 December 2007
Written by: Russell T Davies

The bow of a ship crashes through the wall of the TARDIS, its name, *Titanic*! Repairing the TARDIS walls and pushing the ship out again, the Doctor lands the TARDIS on board. The *Titanic* is actually a luxury space-cruiser from the planet Sto that is currently orbiting Earth on Christmas Eve 2007.

The Doctor stows away to enjoy the party and meets Astrid Peth, a waitress with a desire to see the stars. During a visit to the planet's surface, they meet newspaper seller Wilfred Mott. Once the excursion party is back on board, the ship is hit by meteors while the shields are offline.

As the *Titanic* plummets towards Earth, the Doctor leads a group of survivors through the ship, while the Hosts – angelic android servitors – attempt to eliminate them. He discovers that the person controlling the Hosts – and the one who paid the Captain to take the shields offline – is Max Capricorn, the cruise line's cyborg owner, who is seeking revenge against the company's board of directors for forcing him out.

Astrid saves the Doctor, killing Capricorn and herself in the process. The Doctor heads to the bridge and helps Midshipman Frame restart the engines just before the ship hits Buckingham Palace.

69
Partners in Crime

An adventure for:	Tenth Doctor and Donna
First shown:	5 April 2008
Written by:	Russell T Davies

After their first meeting in *The Runaway Bride*, Donna Noble tries to find the Doctor again by investigating unusual events, in the hope that the Doctor will also be interested. Sure enough, they both independently investigate Adipose Industries, a company claiming to offer a miraculous weight-loss product. But actually, the company is run by the alien Miss Foster. She is using the product to create millions of Adipose children for the Adiposian First Family, who have lost their breeding planet. The Adipose are made out of the excess body fat of people who take the treatment.

When she realises that the Doctor is about to warn the Shadow Proclamation about her illegal activities on Earth, Miss Foster activates an Inducer. This will start the process of creating millions of Adipose using not just excess fat but the entire bodies of everyone using the Adipose products.

As thousands of Adipose are created and hurry towards Adipose Industries, the Doctor and Donna manage to stop the Inducer. The thousands of Adipose that have been created are picked up by a huge spaceship, and Miss Foster is killed by the Adiposians so she cannot incriminate them. The Doctor arranges for the Shadow Proclamation to take the Adipose children into care and invites a delighted Donna to join him on his travels.

RIGHT: Illustration by Julia Traband

70
The Fires of Pompeii

An adventure for:	Tenth Doctor and Donna
First shown:	12 April 2008
Written by:	James Moran

The Doctor plans to take Donna to ancient Rome. But they actually arrive in Pompeii in AD 79, just as Mount Vesuvius is about to erupt. Strange things are already happening in Pompeii – it seems that the augurs and soothsayers really can see the future (except for the imminent volcanic eruption), and they are slowly turning to stone.

The Doctor and Donna discover that a group of aliens called Pyrovile aliens has arrived under the mountain. Escaping from the destruction of their home world Pyrovilia, the creatures are made of rock and fire. All their technology is also derived from these elements. They plan to weld themselves to humans, boiling away Earth's seas and oceans to create a new world for themselves.

The only way the Doctor and Donna can save the world is by sacrificing Pompeii and its citizens. They invert the Pyroviles' systems, turning the power of the volcano back against them. As history later records, Vesuvius erupts with the force of twenty-four nuclear bombs. The Doctor and Donna are saved by a Pyrovile escape pod, and Donna persuades the Doctor to rescue one family from Pompeii.

RIGHT: Illustration by Christina Anderson

71

Silence in the Library/ Forest of the Dead

An adventure for:	Tenth Doctor and Donna
First shown:	31 May–7 June 2008 (2 episodes)
Written by:	Steven Moffat

The Doctor and Donna arrive in the Library – a vast complex that covers an entire planet. But they find it deserted and in shadows. They meet up with an expedition organised by Strackman Lux to discover what's happened. The Library computer, CAL, insists that everyone was saved, but the Doctor discovers the Library is infested with Vashta Nerada – 'piranhas of the air' that imitate shadows and strip the flesh from their victims in seconds.

The Doctor discovers that the Vashta Nerada hatched from the books in the Library – the paper being made from trees where the creatures laid their spores. Meanwhile, Donna is trapped in a virtual world, living out an ideal life with a husband and children.

It turns out that CAL is actually the digitised mind of a little girl – Charlotte – and has saved Donna and the other missing people into the computer itself. The Doctor agrees to give the Vashta Nerada the run of the Library in return for them allowing everyone to leave safely – but most of the expedition is killed during the course of events, living on only within the world simulated by CAL. This includes the mysterious River Song, who seems to know so much about the Doctor even though he has never met her before.

LEFT: Illustration by Megan Manning

RIGHT: Illustration by Amarina Van Nunen

72 Midnight

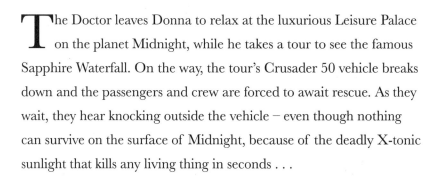

An adventure for:	Tenth Doctor and Donna
First shown:	14 June 2008
Written by:	Russell T Davies

The Doctor leaves Donna to relax at the luxurious Leisure Palace on the planet Midnight, while he takes a tour to see the famous Sapphire Waterfall. On the way, the tour's Crusader 50 vehicle breaks down and the passengers and crew are forced to await rescue. As they wait, they hear knocking outside the vehicle – even though nothing can survive on the surface of Midnight, because of the deadly X-tonic sunlight that kills any living thing in seconds . . .

When the knocking stops, Sky – one of the passengers – starts to behave strangely. The Doctor realises that she has been possessed by the strange life form from outside. Sky repeats everything anyone says. Soon she is speaking at the same time as the others. Finally, she fixes on the Doctor as her target and pre-empts his speech before stealing his voice completely, leaving him only able to repeat what she says . . .

Most of the passengers now believe that the Doctor is the real threat and turn against him. But the tour's hostess – who realises Sky is the one possessed – destroys the mysterious Midnight Entity by ejecting herself and Sky out of the vehicle, where they are both vaporised by the X-tonic sunlight.

RIGHT: Illustration by Bela Belistic

73
Turn Left

An adventure for:	Tenth Doctor and Donna
First shown:	21 June 2008
Written by:	Russell T Davies

In the market on planet Shan Shen, Donna visits a strange fortune teller, and her past life changes. She doesn't realise that it has been altered by a Time Beetle – one of the mysterious Trickster's Brigade . . .

The Time Beetle latches on to a moment when Donna made a seemingly trivial but actually vital decision. She took a left turn in her car to go for a job interview that eventually led to her meeting the Doctor. The Time Beetle alters Donna's life history so that she turned right instead. This means that Donna never met the Doctor, and without Donna's help, the Doctor then died after defeating the Empress of the Racnoss in *The Runaway Bride*.

Without the Doctor, events he prevented actually take place, and eventually the fabric of the Universe begins to collapse. In the alternate history, Donna meets Rose Tyler, who persuades Donna to go back in time to change her decision. But she doesn't get there in time, and ends up throwing herself under a car to create a traffic jam, causing her past self to turn left to avoid it. As Donna is dying, Rose gives her a message to pass on to the Doctor.

Finding herself back in the 'real' world of the Shan Shen market, the Time Beetle falls off Donna's back and she is freed from its influence. She tells the Doctor about meeting a blonde woman, whom the Doctor recognises as having been Rose. When Donna says Rose sent the message 'Bad Wolf', the Doctor is horror-struck, saying it means the end of the Universe.

RIGHT: Illustration by
Helen-Lorraine Tope

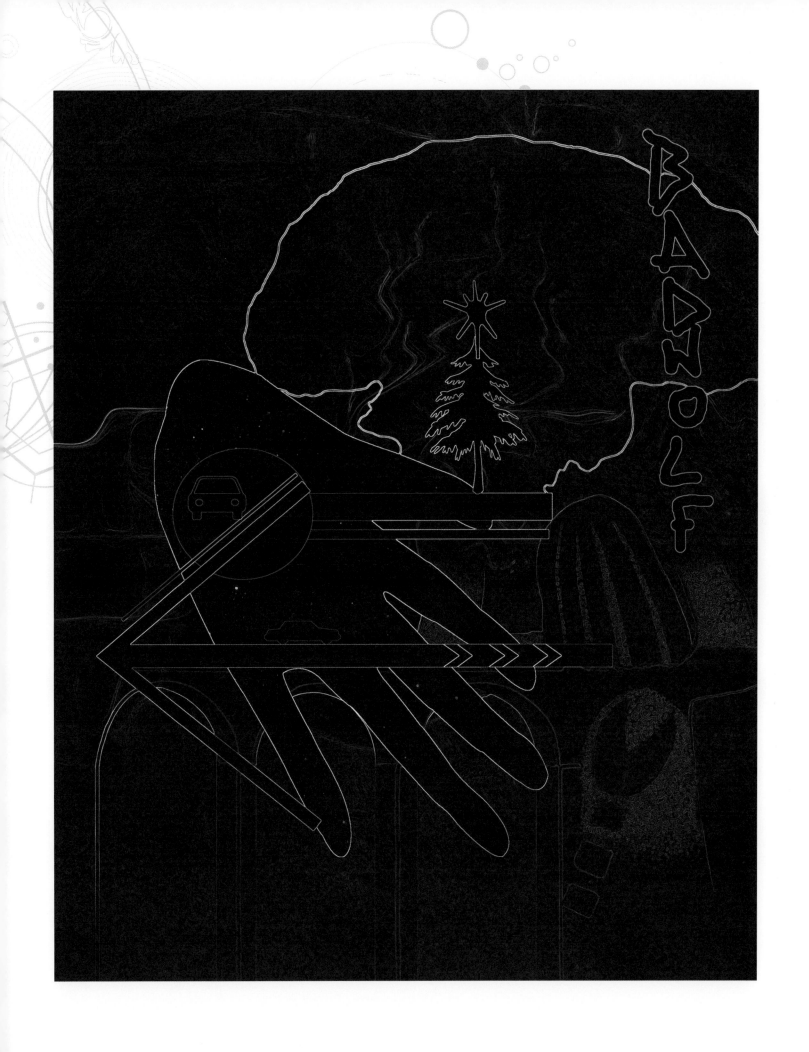

74
The Stolen Earth/Journey's End

An adventure for: Tenth Doctor and Donna
First shown: 28 June–5 July 2008 (2 episodes)
Written by: Russell T Davies

ABOVE: Illustration by Thomas McKenzie Went

The Daleks have stolen the Earth and transported it across space to the furthest reaches of the Medusa Cascade, along with 26 other planets. These Daleks have been re-created by Davros, the Kaled scientist who first invented the Daleks on the planet Skaro. He has been saved from the Time War by Dalek Caan, one of the Cult of Skaro. Davros and the Daleks plan to use the powerful configuration of planets they have created to provide energy for the ultimate weapon – the Reality Bomb.

The Doctor and his friends are held captive by Davros. But a second Doctor is created when the Doctor is shot by a Dalek, and channels regenerative energy into the hand severed in his fight with the Sycorax Leader many adventures previously. Caught up in the regeneration process, Donna is made part Time Lord, just as this new Doctor is part human. Donna manages to defeat the Daleks, but at a terrible cost: the Doctor has to wipe Donna's memories of him for her to survive.

With Davros defeated, the 'new' Doctor stays with Rose Tyler in the parallel universe where she lives.

75

The Waters of Mars

An adventure for: Tenth Doctor and Adelaide

First shown: 15 November 2009

Written by: Russell T Davies and Phil Ford

The TARDIS arrives on Mars in 2059. The Doctor stumbles across Bowie Base One, the first human outpost on the Red Planet. He is detained by a robot called Gadget and brought before Commander Adelaide Brooke. The Doctor realises that this is a fixed point in time – the day, according to history, when the base is destroyed killing of all the crew. He tries to leave so that he doesn't affect the timeline, but a developing crisis prevents it. One of the crew has been infected by an alien life form that takes over his body, causing water to gush from his mouth. Brooke suspects the Doctor of having caused the infection.

ABOVE: Illustration by Lia England-Lonsway

More of the team become hosts for the life form. The Flood, as it is called, desires to reach Earth, a planet rich in water. As the situation becomes untenable, the Doctor and Brooke use Gadget to escape the infected crew members.

The Doctor discovers that the alien virus had been trapped in a glacier by the Ice Warriors to prevent its spread. When humans melted the glacier to provide the base with a water supply, it was freed again.

To prevent the Flood from reaching Earth, Brooke prepares to detonate a nuclear device at the heart of the base. The Doctor takes the survivors on board the TARDIS and back to Earth. However, understanding that the Doctor has tampered with a fixed point in time to save her, Brooke commits suicide in order to keep history on course.

76

The End of Time

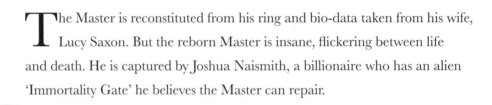

An adventure for:	Tenth Doctor and Wilf
First shown:	25 December 2009–1 January 2010 (2 episodes)
Written by:	Russell T Davies

The Master is reconstituted from his ring and bio-data taken from his wife, Lucy Saxon. But the reborn Master is insane, flickering between life and death. He is captured by Joshua Naismith, a billionaire who has an alien 'Immortality Gate' he believes the Master can repair.

The Doctor tracks down the Master. But he is too late to stop him using the Gate to project versions of himself into every human being on Earth – soon, *everyone* becomes the Master.

The Master's madness is a result of the Time Lords creating a link between the last days of the Great Time War and the present – so that they can escape the Time Lock that keeps them trapped on Gallifrey. They travel down the link, and use the Gate to manifest themselves on Earth. But if they are successful, Gallifrey and the horrors of the Time War will also escape, so the Doctor and Master together close the link. The Master is killed, but the Time Lock is restored.

All seems well – but Wilf is trapped inside the Gate's isolation chamber, about to be killed by a flood of deadly radiation. To save Wilf, the Doctor takes his place. As the radiation destroys his body, he says farewell to many of his recent companions before he returns to the TARDIS and regenerates . . .

RIGHT: Illustration by Coll Hamilton

77
The Eleventh Hour

An adventure for: Eleventh Doctor, Amy and Rory
First shown: 3 April 2010
Written by: Steven Moffat

The newly regenerated Eleventh Doctor crash-lands the TARDIS in the garden of little Amelia Pond. He strikes up a friendship with Amelia, but then accidentally goes forward in time eleven years – meeting her again as a young woman, now calling herself Amy.

Amy waited for her 'Raggedy Doctor', who everyone said was her imaginary friend, and can't quite believe he has come back. His reappearance coincides with the escape of Prisoner Zero through a crack in Amy's bedroom wall – a crack in the fabric of the Universe. Prisoner Zero's jailers, the Atraxi, are also hunting for him – and will destroy Earth if they have to in order to prevent the prisoner's escape.

With the help of Amy's friend Rory Williams, the Doctor tracks Prisoner Zero to the local

hospital. He exposes Prisoner Zero to the Atraxi who take him prisoner.

ABOVE: Illustration by Anna Schwarz

Two years later, the Doctor returns again for Amy – and she joins him in the TARDIS to travel through time and space. She doesn't tell the Doctor that tomorrow is her wedding day . . .

RIGHT: Illustration by Andy Williams

78
Vincent and the Doctor

An adventure for:	Eleventh Doctor and Amy
First shown:	5 June 2010
Written by:	Richard Curtis

Visiting an exhibition of paintings by Van Gogh, the Doctor is intrigued to see the face of a monster at the window of a church in one of the paintings. What did Van Gogh see? The only way to find out is to go and ask him. So the Doctor takes Amy back to Arles in 1890, where they meet the painter himself and soon befriend him.

The creature is an invisible Krafayis, stranded on Earth and attacking the local population. The Doctor rigs up a device that lets him see the Krafayis, but Van Gogh – who perceives the world in a different way from other people – can already see it.

Knowing the Krafayis will be at the church in the painting when Van Gogh paints it, the Doctor and Amy corner the creature with Vincent's help. To the Doctor's great sadness, the creature, which is blind and frightened, is killed in the chase.

The Doctor and Amy take Van Gogh – who is racked with self-doubt and depression – to the future in the TARDIS to see the exhibition of his paintings. Vincent is moved to hear the curator extolling his work, though sadly, it does not prevent the painter from soon taking his own life.

RIGHT: Illustration by Zena Wood

79
The Pandorica Opens/ The Big Bang

An adventure for:	Eleventh Doctor, Amy and Rory
First shown:	19–26 June 2011 (2 episodes)
Written by:	Steven Moffat

An alliance of the Doctor's greatest enemies has set a trap for him. The Pandorica is a myth, a legend, said to contain a great warrior. Drawn to Roman Britain by River Song, the Doctor and Amy discover the Pandorica underneath Stonehenge, guarded by a damaged Cyberman. Amy is saved from the Cyberman by Rory, who should be dead, but has returned as a Roman centurion.

In fact, this Rory is an Auton, created from Amy's memories. Amy herself is part of the trap, but Auton-Rory kills her. The Doctor is captured and imprisoned inside the Pandorica, which turns out to have been a prison designed for him all along. He manages to escape, and places Amy's injured body inside.

In 1996, with the Universe ending because of a mysterious crack in the framework of reality, young Amy finds the Pandorica as part of a museum exhibition. Inside, her older self has recovered – and Auton-Rory is still waiting for her.

ABOVE: Illustration by Josh J. Ford

Together with River Song, the Doctor, Amy and Rory battle against a stone Dalek and manage to avert the end of the Universe. But it seems the Doctor was killed in the process – until he arrives at Amy and Rory's wedding.

80

The Impossible Astronaut/ The Day of the Moon

An adventure for:	Eleventh Doctor, Amy and Rory
First shown:	23–30 April 2011 (2 episodes)
Written by:	Steven Moffat

ABOVE: Illustration by Ng Cheuk Tone

RIGHT: Illustration by Daniel Cheeseman

The Doctor summons Amy, Rory and River Song to meet him in the Utah desert. An astronaut appears miraculously from a lake, wearing a NASA spacesuit, and kills the Doctor – blasting him down repeatedly so that he cannot regenerate. The Doctor is dead.

Devastated, Amy, Rory and River are astonished when they meet the Doctor again – but this is an earlier Doctor, who has no idea of what will happen to him. Travelling back to 1969, they all meet President Nixon, who is receiving mysterious phone calls from a little girl pleading for his help. Tracing the girl, who it seems might one day become the mysterious 'impossible' astronaut, the

Doctor discovers that Earth has already been secretly invaded by the Silence – grotesque humanoid creatures that people forget as soon as they look away.

With the help of US agent Canton Delaware, the Doctor and his friends evade the Silence, though Amy is captured. The Doctor uses TV coverage of the *Apollo 11* moon landing to implant a subliminal message in all of humanity to drive out the Silence.

But questions remain – will the Doctor really die? Why is Amy hallucinating about a woman with an eye patch? And who is the little girl who it seems can regenerate?

81
The Doctor's Wife

An adventure for:	Eleventh Doctor, Amy and Rory
First shown:	14 May 2011
Written by:	Neil Gaiman

The Doctor gets a thought message from another Time Lord – the Corsair. Despite the risk, he follows in the hope of rescuing his colleague. He follows the signal to an asteroid covered in junk within a small bubble universe. Here the Doctor, Amy and Rory meet the strange Auntie, Uncle and Nephew (who is an Ood). But the message turns out to be a trap. The asteroid itself, a strange being called House, sent it, having already killed the Corsair and many other Time Lords.

To spring the trap, House transfers the TARDIS's matrix into a woman. Disoriented and calling herself Idris, she befriends the Doctor, who gradually realises that she is his TARDIS in human form.

Amy and Rory are trapped aboard the TARDIS, which has been taken over by the mind of House. But the Doctor and Idris manage to build a small TARDIS from the junk on the asteroid – bits of other TARDISes that House has discarded. They use the makeshift TARDIS console to land in the secondary control room of the Doctor's TARDIS. Idris's body is failing, but as she dies she releases the matrix back into the TARDIS, destroying House in the process.

RIGHT: Illustration by Chloe Rose

82
The Girl Who Waited

An adventure for: Eleventh Doctor, Amy and Rory
First shown: 10 September 2011
Written by: Steven Moffat

Amy and Rory go with the Doctor to Apalapucia, a holiday resort planet, not realising it is under quarantine. Amy gets separated from the Doctor and Rory into a different time stream. A Handbot welcomes the Doctor and Rory to the Two Streams Facility for victims of the Chen-7 one-day plague, which affects two-hearted races, while Amy is trapped in a faster time stream that the others cannot access.

Boarding the TARDIS again, the Doctor and Rory manage to land in Amy's time stream, but discover that she has been waiting for them for thirty-six years. In that time she has built her own sonic probe and grown to hate the Time Lord. The Doctor uses the facility's temporal engines to fold the two points of Amy's timeline together. Because of the Chen-7 plague he is unable to leave the TARDIS so Rory goes after Amy alone.

The Doctor promises to let the older Amy travel with her younger self aboard the TARDIS. However, because of

the massive paradox this would cause, the TARDIS starts to malfunction. The older Amy fights off the Handbots pursuing them, allowing Rory and the younger Amy to board the time machine. The older Amy is left outside, suffering the Handbots' 'kindness' as the others leave.

ABOVE: Illustration by Stephanie Jackson

83
The Angels Take Manhattan

An adventure for:	Eleventh Doctor, River, Amy and Rory
First shown:	29 September 2012
Written by:	Steven Moffat

In 2012, in New York City, the Doctor, Amy and Rory are having a picnic in Central Park. The Doctor is reading a pulp paperback novel about a private detective called Melody Malone.

On his way back from getting more coffee, Rory is sent back to 1938 by a Weeping Angel cherub. Continuing to read the novel, the Doctor realises that Rory has been transported back in time, so he and Amy set off in pursuit in the TARDIS.

In 1938, Rory meets Melody Malone – who turns out to be River Song. They are taken to the home of art collector and mob boss Julius Grayle, who has a chained and damaged Weeping Angel in his mansion. Grayle demands River tell him everything she knows about the Angels. Meanwhile, Rory is attacked by stone cherubs in the mansion's basement . . .

ABOVE: Illustration by Markee Shadows

The TARDIS lands in 1938, where the Doctor and Amy find River at Grayle's mansion before locating Rory at Winter Quay, a Weeping Angels' battery farm. There, Amy meets Rory's older self and holds his hand as he passes away. Heading to the roof, the group are confronted by a snarling Statue of Liberty, also now a Weeping Angel.

In order to create a paradox, which would poison the time energy the Angels feed on and kill them, Rory commits suicide with Amy, by jumping off the roof. The plan works and the party wake up in a cemetery in New York, back in 2012. But just as everyone boards the TARDIS, Rory is sent back in time by a surviving Angel, – and Amy allows herself to be sent back too, to be with him.

84

The Snowmen

An adventure for: Eleventh Doctor and Clara
First shown: 25 December 2012
Written by: Steven Moffat

In 1842, a boy builds a snowman that speaks to him – and in 1892, at the Great Intelligence Institute, Dr Walter Simeon collects snow samples, placing them in a large glass sphere. The voice he heard fifty years before now addresses him from the snow globe, heralding the end of humanity.

Elsewhere in Victorian London, a barmaid called Clara asks the Doctor if he made a snowman that has appeared outside as if from nowhere. He inspects it, before leaving in a carriage driven by the Sontaran Strax. Clara climbs aboard too.

Strax, Madame Vastra – a Silurian integrated into Victorian London life – and her human servant/wife Jenny are allies of the Doctor known as the Paternoster Gang. Vastra and Jenny confront Simeon and when he tells them that they cannot stop him, Vastra tells him that they know someone who can.

Disembarking from the carriage, the Doctor and Clara are attacked by animated snowmen. The Doctor teaches Clara to defend herself by imagining them melting. Following him again, climbing a staircase into the sky, Clara finds the TARDIS resting on a cloud.

On Christmas Eve, Clara returns to her other job as governess to the Latimer children. They are attacked by an ice imitation of their former governess. The Paternoster Gang protect the family while Clara and the Doctor deal with the ice governess.

In their final confrontation with Simeon, the Intelligence from the globe takes over his empty mind. Clara, fatally injured during the encounter with the ice governess, dies. Realising that she is the same woman he 'met' in the Dalek Asylum, the Doctor sets off to find out who she is.

RIGHT: Illustration by Allison Stidham

85
The Rings of Akhaten

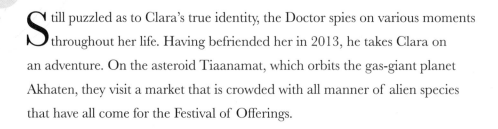

An adventure for:	Eleventh Doctor and Clara
First shown:	6 April 2013
Written by:	Neil Cross

Still puzzled as to Clara's true identity, the Doctor spies on various moments throughout her life. Having befriended her in 2013, he takes Clara on an adventure. On the asteroid Tiaanamat, which orbits the gas-giant planet Akhaten, they visit a market that is crowded with all manner of alien species that have all come for the Festival of Offerings.

Clara meets an alien child called Merry Galel, who is actually Tiaanamat's Queen of Years, and who was chosen to sing in the festival when she was a baby. Merry is scared because she has to sing to prevent her planet's dormant and malevolent Old God from waking.

Clara and the Doctor watch the ceremony together as Merry sings the lullaby, called the Long Song, as part of a duet with the Chorister. However, when the Chorister falters, Merry is drawn towards the Pyramid of the Sun-Singers.

The Doctor and Clara set off on an anti-grav moped to save her. It turns out that the gas giant Akhaten itself is the Old God. To stop the parasitic, sentient planet from destroying the Universe, Clara feeds it a leaf that represents her mother's lost life. The infinite possibilities it symbolises are too much for Akhaten, and the planet recedes, asleep now for good.

RIGHT: Illustration by Marie Foulquie

86
The Name of the Doctor

An adventure for:	Eleventh Doctor and Clara
First shown:	18 May 2013
Written by:	Steven Moffat

By means of a psychic conference call across time, the Paternoster Gang, Clara and River discuss the information Madame Vastra received from the Whispermen via a condemned murderer. They have been given the coordinates for Trenzalore, the planet where the Doctor is doomed to die.

The Paternoster Gang are then kidnapped by the Whispermen, and the Doctor and Clara are forced to travel to Trenzalore to save them, even though the risks involved in the Time Lord visiting his own future are huge. At the centre of a vast graveyard, where those who fell during the Doctor's last battle are buried, they find the Doctor's tomb – his TARDIS grown to an enormous size.

Inside the control room of the dying TARDIS, the Doctor and the Great Intelligence (in the form of Dr Simeon) have their final confrontation. The Great Intelligence enters the Doctor's timeline, rewriting his entire history, until Clara enters the rift as well, undoing all the damage the alien entity has done.

With the Great Intelligence defeated, the Doctor risks everything by entering his own time stream to get Clara back.

In a dark, cavernous space, Clara sees thirteen incarnations of the Doctor, finally coming face to face with the War Doctor, too.

RIGHT: Illustration by Marianne Mosquera

There's no need to
actually hold my hand.
JOURNAL
mind is
Cross
my
Hearts

87
The Day of the Doctor

An adventure for: Eleventh Doctor, Tenth Doctor, War Doctor and Clara
First shown: 23 November 2013
Written by: Steven Moffat

After the TARDIS is airlifted by helicopter to the National Gallery in London, Kate Lethbridge-Stewart – UNIT's Chief Scientific Officer – shows the Doctor and Clara an impossible 3D painting called 'Gallifrey Falls'. The Doctor recognises it as a piece of Gallifreyan art, a slice of frozen time, from the fall of Arcadia.

On the final day of the Time War, the War Doctor prepares to activate the Moment, a weapon that has the power to wipe out both sides in the conflict – Daleks and Time Lords. The Moment's consciousness manifests in the form of Rose Tyler, declaring that the Doctor's punishment for committing genocide shall be to survive, and opening a time fissure to show him his future.

The fissure also opens in the National Gallery in the Eleventh Doctor's timeline. He steps through into sixteenth-century England, where the Tenth Doctor is struggling to work out which of two Elizabeth the Firsts is the real one, and which a Zygon impostor. The War

Doctor joins them, but is unimpressed by his future selves. The three Doctors are then arrested by the Queen's guards and taken to the Tower of London.

In 2013, Kate takes Clara to the Black Archive where dangerous alien artefacts are stored, including a vortex manipulator . . .

The Doctors learn that the Zygons are using stasis cubes to insert themselves into the 3D paintings, so that they might emerge in the future when Earth has become more technologically advanced. Clara rescues the Time Lords from the past, but they discover that in the present the Zygons have already infiltrated the Black Archive.

Travelling back to the present day via a 3D painting, the Doctors force the humans and Zygons to reach a peaceful resolution. The Moment then transports all three incarnations to Gallifrey, where the Eleventh Doctor comes up with the idea of freezing the planet in time, thus saving his home from destruction.

ABOVE: Illustration by Marie Foulquie

LEFT: Illustration by Jessica Baynes

ABOVE: Illustration by Jon Wilson

ABOVE: Illustration by Chris Embleton-Hall

88
Deep Breath

An adventure for:	Twelfth Doctor and Clara
First shown:	23 August 2014
Written by:	Steven Moffat

ABOVE: Illustration by Elizabeth Cavanagh

The newly-regenerated Doctor, temporarily forgetting how to pilot the TARDIS, has accidentally been swallowed in his time machine by a T. rex. The dinosaur is taken along with the TARDIS when it makes the jump to Victorian London, where the Paternoster Gang help the Doctor and Clara adjust to his new incarnation.

The dinosaur is soon killed by spontaneous combustion, which the Doctor discovers is just one of several such incidents of late. He visits Mancini's Family Restaurant, where he is joined by Clara. Ending up in a chamber beneath the restaurant, they meet the Half-Face Man and discover that 'he' is actually a servitor robot from the SS *Marie Antoinette*.

It and the other robots crashed on Earth millions of years ago, after the ship fell through time, and have been rebuilding themselves over and over again ever since, now using human body parts.

As the Paternoster Gang fight off the other robots, the Doctor and the Half-Face Man end up battling aboard an escape pod that has been turned into a hot-air balloon with an envelope made from human skin. Ultimately, the cyborg plunges to its death, impaled on the spire of Big Ben.

The Doctor's regeneration having stabilised, he reconciles with Clara, saying he wishes to put right the many mistakes he has made in the past.

RIGHT: Illustration by Catherine Smith

89
Robot of Sherwood

An adventure for:	Twelfth Doctor and Clara
First shown:	6 September 2014
Written by:	Mark Gatiss

Clara asks to meet Robin Hood, even though the Doctor does not believe he ever actually existed. Travelling to Sherwood Forest in 1190, they are surprised to meet the legendary outlaw in the flesh, although the Doctor can't quite believe Robin isn't really a robotic creation or similar.

Both Robin and the Doctor enter an archery contest at Nottingham Castle. Winning the competition, the Doctor discards the golden arrow that is the prize, asking the Sheriff for enlightenment instead. The Sheriff orders his knights to seize Robin, the Doctor and Clara, and in the ensuing battle Robin chops off a knight's arm, revealing it to be a robot.

The robots are from the twenty-ninth century and their spaceship now lies at the heart of Nottingham Castle, having crashed on Earth on its way to the Promised Land. They are collecting gold to repair the vessel's damaged circuits.

With Clara's help, the Doctor frees Maid Marian and a group of peasants from the castle dungeons, Robin defeats the Sheriff, and the merry band escapes as the knights' ship takes off. Shooting the golden arrow from the archery contest into the ship's engines, they give it the boost it needs to reach orbit, at which point it explodes, without causing any harm to those left on the ground.

RIGHT: Illustration by Bethan Applegarth

90
Listen

An adventure for:	Twelfth Doctor and Clara
First shown:	13 September 2014
Written by:	Steven Moffat

While talking to himself, the Doctor ponders why people talk to themselves, which leads him to wonder whether a creature ever evolved with the perfect ability to hide.

After a disastrous date with Danny Pink, Clara joins the Doctor on board the TARDIS as he tests his hypothesis. He plugs her into the TARDIS's telepathic circuits, which takes them to a children's home in Gloucester in the 1990s. There they meet Rupert Pink, a boy who is afraid of being alone. While Clara is showing him that there's nothing lurking under his bed, something sits on top of it. The Doctor realises that whatever it is hiding under the bedspread wants to stay hidden. They all stare out of the window so that it can leave unseen.

Getting the Doctor to take her back to the restaurant so that she can try to patch things up with Danny (which doesn't go well), Clara then meets Orson Pink, a time traveller from one hundred years in the future. The Doctor found him on the last planet in the Universe, after searching Clara's timeline again, and takes them back there. Orson is terrified of something that he believes is waiting in the dark outside his capsule.

When the Doctor is knocked unconscious trying to find out what 'it' is, Clara uses the psychic circuits to take them somewhere else, but this time ends up on Gallifrey in the Doctor's past. She meets the child who will become the Doctor and tells him – repeating the words the Doctor had earlier told Rupert – that fear can be a superpower.

RIGHT: Illustration by David North

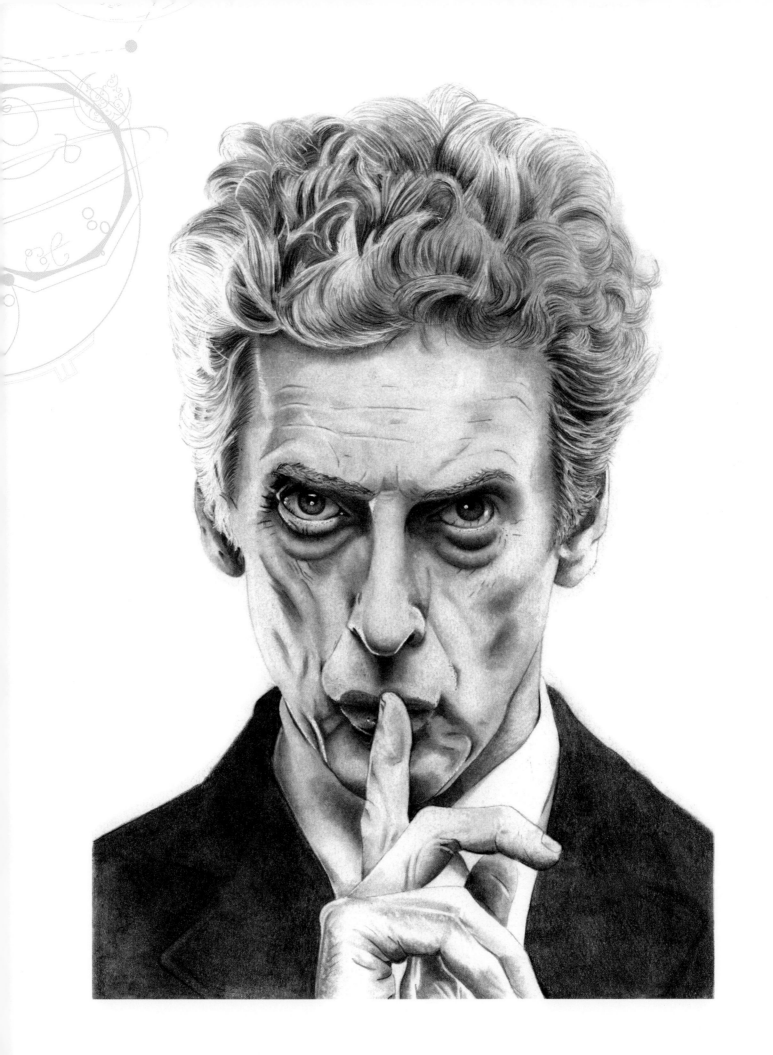

91
Mummy on the Orient Express

An adventure for: Twelfth Doctor and Clara
First shown: 11 October 2014
Written by: Jamie Mathieson

The TARDIS lands on board a space-faring version of the Orient Express. As they enjoy all that the dining car has to offer, it becomes clear that Clara has told the Doctor that this will be their last trip together.

The Doctor is intrigued to learn of the death of Mrs Pitt, one of the passengers, apparently at the hand of a mummy that only she could see. Investigating further he meets Perkins, the chief engineer, who tells him other deaths have occurred aboard the train.

One Professor Emile Moorhouse tells the Doctor about a mythical mummy called the Foretold. Quell, the captain of the train, believes that the Doctor is responsible for the deaths and arrests him, but the Doctor realises that the

Orient Express cruise was arranged to find out more about the Foretold; Gus, the train's computer, confirms his suspicions.

The Time Lord deduces that the Foretold is an ancient soldier, augmented with stealth technology, and is killing the passengers because it believes the war it fought in is still ongoing. With the Foretold about to kill him, the Doctor surrenders. The soldier stops and, relieved of duty, turns to dust.

Gus destroys the train, as no survivors are required, but the Doctor is able to teleport all the passengers into the TARDIS and take them to the nearest civilised planet. Impressed by his kindness, Clara decides to keep travelling with the Doctor.

RIGHT: Illustration by Alice Carnegie

THE LAST HURRAH

92
Flatline

An adventure for:	Twelfth Doctor and Clara
First shown:	18 October 2014
Written by:	Jamie Mathieson

Attempting to return Clara home, the Doctor lands the TARDIS in Bristol and discovers that the vessel's exterior dimensions have shrunk, its power being drained by something nearby. The Doctor remains inside while Clara investigates outside. She discovers locals are disappearing, with strange murals of them appearing on the walls of an underpass.

Returning to the TARDIS, Clara finds it has shrunk still further, trapping the Doctor inside. Carrying the TARDIS with her, and using the Doctor's psychic paper and sonic screwdriver, Clara poses as Dr Oswald and joins forces with local graffiti artist Rigsy to find out what's going on.

The recent disappearances are down to entities from a two-dimensional universe. The 2D creatures pursue Clara, Rigsy and a group of community service workers, while the Doctor creates a device that restores three dimensions in order to fight them.

Soon, the Doctor is forced to activate the TARDIS's siege mode. Clara then cleverly tricks the creatures into feeding dimensional energy into the TARDIS, restoring it to normal. The Doctor emerges and banishes the Boneless, as he christens the creatures, using his sonic to send them back to their own dimension.

LEFT: Illustration by Angelica Botero

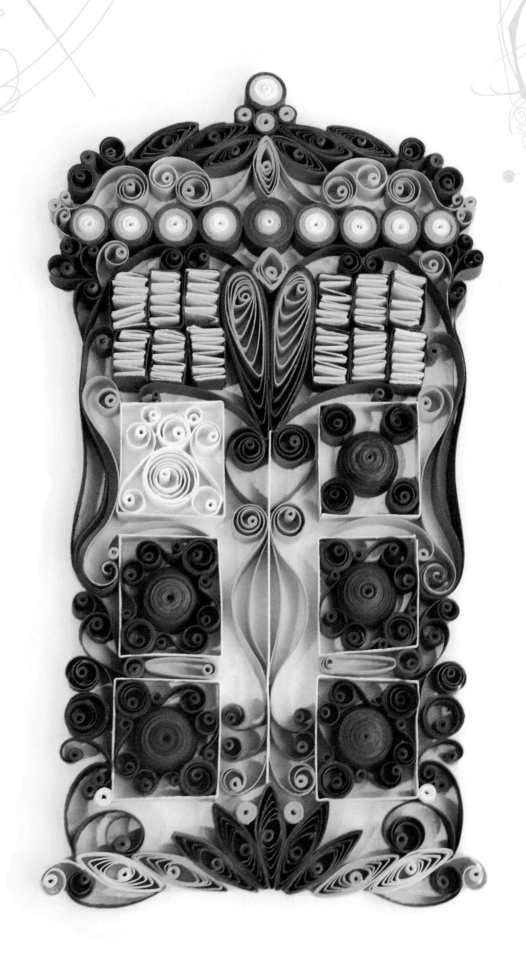

93
The Zygon Invasion/
The Zygon Inversion

An adventure for:	Twelfth Doctor and Clara
First shown:	31 October–7 November 2015 (2 episodes)
Written by:	Peter Harness and Steven Moffat

Osgood sends the Doctor the message 'Nightmare Scenario', which he knows means that the truce he established between the Zygon race and the human race has broken down. Travelling to a park on Earth, he meets the Zygon high command – which has taken the form of two little girls – but they are soon captured by the Zygon splinter group Truth or Consequences.

The Doctor visits UNIT to acquire more resources and discovers that the splinter group are holding Osgood hostage in order to find out more about something called the Osgood Box. Kate Stewart explains that since the ceasefire there have been two Osgoods – one human, one Zygon. The Doctor invokes his powers as President of Earth and travels on his presidential plane, Boat One, to Turmezistan to find Osgood and prevent a war between the Zygons and the humans.

Clara is captured and replaced by a Zygon double calling itself Bonnie, who tries to shoot Boat One out of the sky – but the Doctor and Osgood parachute to safety.

Because she looks like Clara, Bonnie gains access to the Black Archive and discovers there are actually two Osgood boxes – one that will expose all the Zygons currently passing as human, and one that will kill them. Kate Stewart, the Doctor and Osgood enter the archive to confront Bonnie.

With a striking speech on the subject of war, the Doctor manages to talk Bonnie round and, once he's wiped everyone's memory – apart from Bonnie's – she returns to her nest, informing her fellow Zygons that the revolution is over and they are safe. The Doctor invites Osgood to travel with him but she declines, preferring to stay on Earth to make sure the Nightmare Scenario doesn't happen again.

ABOVE: Illustration by Adam Howling

94
Face the Raven

An adventure for:	Twelfth Doctor and Clara
First shown:	21 November 2015
Written by:	Sarah Dollard

The Doctor and Clara receive a call from Rigsy; a tattoo has appeared on the back of his neck, which is counting down to zero, and he has no memory of the previous twenty-four hours. The Doctor discovers that Rigsy has been in contact with alien life and will die when the countdown ends.

Trying to help him piece together his movements over the last day, while looking at maps of London, Clara mentions something called a 'trap street'. Finding the street in question, they enter and find it occupied by refugees from various alien species who appear to be human thanks to a telepathic field.

They soon meet Mayor Me (Ashildr, the Viking girl who the Doctor previously made immortal), who explains that Rigsy has been sentenced to death for killing one of the alien refugees. The tattoo is a chronoclock that draws a Quantum Shade to find him at the predetermined time. Believing Rigsy to have been framed for the murder, the Doctor and Clara investigate.

To protect Rigsy, Clara takes the chronoclock from him, but too late realises that the situation has all been a set-up to trap the Doctor. The countdown reaches zero and the Quantum Shade – appearing in the form of a raven – kills Clara moments before the Doctor is teleported away.

RIGHT: Illustration by Emily Morgan

95
Heaven Sent

An adventure for:	Twelfth Doctor
First shown:	28 November 2015
Written by:	Steven Moffat

As the gears turn inside ancient stone walls, the Doctor materialises inside a teleporter, inside a chamber, inside a castle, in the middle of the sea. The memory of Clara's death fresh in his mind, he swears that he will never stop until he finds the one responsible for bringing him to this place.

Exploring his environment, he discovers that he is in the central tower of the mysterious castle, and realises that he can't have travelled further than one light year. Further exploration leads to him finding a shovel covered in dirt, before realising that he is being pursued by a sinister figure, formed from a childhood nightmare, called the Veil.

Cornered, the Doctor admits that he's afraid of dying, causing the Veil to freeze and the walls and corridors of the castle to rotate, opening a new way forward. This game of cat-and-mouse continues until it becomes apparent that the Doctor has been repeating the same cycle of actions over and over again for millennia.

The Doctor realises that the Time Lords want to know what he knows about a creature called the Hybrid. Finally punching through a wall of solid Azbantium, after four and a half billion years, the Doctor steps through the opening and on to Gallifrey, realising that he's been trapped inside his own confession dial the entire time. He finally reveals, 'The Hybrid, which is destined to conquer Gallifrey and stand in its ruins, is me.'

RIGHT: Illustration by Carter Anderson

96
Hell Bent

An adventure for:	Twelfth Doctor and Clara
First shown:	5 December 2015
Written by:	Steven Moffat

Crossing the Gallifreyan desert, the Doctor arrives at his childhood home, where a woman he recognises warns him that 'they' will kill him.

The Cloister Bells of the High Council Chamber ring ceaselessly and the Time Lords realise that the Doctor has returned. Ohila of the Sisterhood of Karn arrives unannounced and tells Rassilon the Doctor blames him for the horrors of the Time War.

Rassilon sends his forces against the Doctor, but rather than kill him they join him. Rassilon is banished from Gallifrey, followed by the rest of the High Council.

Feeling the need to talk with an old friend to decide what to do next, the Doctor uses Time Lord technology to freeze the moment before Clara died and bring her to Gallifrey. He then flees with her into the Cloisters, beneath the Capitol.

Evading the Wraiths that protect the Cloisters, the Doctor eventually steals a TARDIS and takes Clara to the remains of Gallifrey at the end of the Universe, where they meet Me again, who is now the last thing in existence. Me proposes that the Doctor and Clara are the Hybrid – true companions who will risk the Universe for one another.

Realising they have come to the end of their journey together, the Doctor intends to erase all memory of himself from Clara's mind, but it is he who ends up losing his memories of her. The Doctor is eventually reunited with his TARDIS, while Clara and Me set off on their own adventure in the other stolen TARDIS, which is stuck looking like an American diner.

RIGHT: Illustration by Owain Carbis

97
The Husbands of River Song

An adventure for:	Twelfth Doctor, River Song and Nardole
First shown:	25 December 2015
Written by:	Steven Moffat

On Christmas Day 5343, on the colony world of Mendorax Dellora, the Doctor meets River Song and her 'husband' King Hydroflax. River wants the Doctor to remove the Halassi Androvar – the most valuable diamond in the Universe – from Hydroflax's brain by removing the king's entire head. However, Hydroflax detaches his own head from his mechanical body, ordering it to kill the others.

Using the TARDIS, River and the Doctor travel to the starship *Harmony and Redemption* in order to sell the diamond to an alien buyer named Scratch. This turns out to be a trap set by Scratch and his people, who worship Hydroflax. But the King's body destroys his head, having been promised the Doctor's head instead by the maître d' of the starship.

When the ship is crippled by a meteor strike, the Doctor and River escape aboard the TARDIS with the diamond, as the *Harmony and Redemption* crashes on the planet Darillium – home to the Singing Towers, and the place where River will spend her final night with the Doctor.

Having caught up with River in his own timeline, the Doctor gives her a present – her own sonic screwdriver. They then spend their last night together on Darillium, where one night lasts twenty-four years.

ABOVE: Illustration by Lisa Sikorski

98

The Return of Doctor Mysterio

An adventure for:	Twelfth Doctor and Nardole
First shown:	25 December 2016
Written by:	Steven Moffat

ABOVE: Illustration by Meg Broom

RIGHT: Illustration by Sandra Schock

One Christmas Eve in New York City in the 1990s, a boy called Grant meets the Doctor, mistaking him for Santa Claus. While the Doctor is showing him a 'time distortion equaliser thingy' on the roof of his apartment building, Grant accidentally swallows the alien gemstone that powers the device. The gem grants an individual his desires and so Grant starts to levitate, because his ultimate wish is to be a superhero.

Years later, the Doctor returns with Nardole to investigate Harmony Shoal – an alien invasion force masquerading as a multinational research company. At their HQ he bumps into Lucy, an undercover reporter also investigating. The trio are discovered by the alien masterminds, before being saved by a masked superhero called the Ghost. What Lucy doesn't know is that the Ghost is really Grant, who has fallen in love with her while working as her nanny, using the Ghost alter-ego to help people with his powers.

It takes the combined powers of the Doctor, the Ghost and UNIT to stop the invasion, to prevent the aliens' ship from crashing into Manhattan Island, and to shut down Harmony Shoal. And in a festive happy ending, Lucy realises that she loves Grant, too.

99
The Pilot

An adventure for:	Twelfth Doctor and Bill
First shown:	15 April 2017
Written by:	Steven Moffat

Bill Potts meets the Doctor in his office at St Luke's University, where he is working as a professor. Despite working in the university canteen rather than being enrolled as a student, Bill loves attending the Doctor's lectures – so much so that he offers to be her personal tutor.

Bill meets a fellow student called Heather, who has a starlike pattern in her eye. She leads Bill to a mysterious puddle, which somehow produces a reversed reflection of whoever looks into it rather than a true mirror image. When Heather vanishes, the Doctor starts to investigate.

Bill is confronted by the puddle, which has taken on Heather's form – and when Bill attempts to flee, it pursues her. The Doctor takes Bill on board the TARDIS to help her escape, first travelling to Australia and then to a planet on the other side of the universe, 23 million years into the future, but nothing deters the puddle-entity from its relentless pursuit.

Finally the Doctor leads the puddle-entity into the deadliest fire in the universe – the middle of the Dalek–Movellan War. The Doctor hypothesises that the puddle is a liquid spaceship. Having chosen Heather to be its pilot, it wants Bill to be its passenger. Bill releases Heather from her promise to never leave Bill behind, and the alien liquid departs.

The Doctor and Bill return to Earth and, after promising to keep the Doctor's secret, Bill becomes his new companion.

RIGHT: Illustration by Dan Green

100
Smile

An adventure for:	Twelfth Doctor and Bill
First shown:	22 April 2017
Written by:	Frank Cottrell-Boyce

Despite promising Nardole that he won't leave Earth and neglect his duty regarding the vault hidden under St Luke's University, the Doctor takes Bill into the future. They travel to the human colony planet Gliese 581 D, where the TARDIS materialises in a vast sea of wheat. Soon the pair encounter a swarm of microbots – the Vardy – which implant communication devices into their ears.

Inside the colonists' empty city, the Doctor and Bill meet the humanoid Emojibots and are given badges that reflect their moods in the form of emojis. Having been fed, they are escorted to a greenhouse, where to their horror they find human skeletons being turned into fertiliser for the crops. Realising these are the remains of the colonists' advance party, Bill and the Doctor stall the Emojibots by smiling at them, but are nonetheless pursued by the Vardy.

The Doctor works out that the city has been built around the spaceship that brought the advance party to the planet.

However, as he sets the spaceship's engine core to blow – intending to destroy the Vardy, thereby stopping them from killing the rest of the colonists when they arrive – he discovers that the colonists are already on board and are starting to wake up.

With the two sides ready to eliminate each other – the Emojibots simply trying to protect the colonists from their own grief, which the robots perceive as a threat to the humans' happiness – the Doctor wipes the Vardy's memories. Having become sentient, they now believe themselves to be the planet's indigenous life form. The Doctor tells the humans that they must negotiate with the Vardy to settle on the planet, as they are now a migrant race seeking asylum.

The Doctor and Bill return to Earth. But when they exit the TARDIS they find themselves standing on a frozen River Thames, with an elephant walking towards them over the ice . . .

RIGHT: Illustration by John Ross and Alan Craddock

With special thanks to . . .

A Shivani
Abbie Bardell
Abby Rose Percy
Abi Newsome
Abigail Stidham
Adam Dunn
Adam Evans
Adam Stoller
Adele Lorienne
Adriana Martinez
Aeryn Moor
Aimee Ford
Aimee Young
Ainsley "Boo" Sullivan
Alan Pickthall
Alasdair Riddell
Albie Sibson-Harris
Alex Jepson
Alex Storer
Alice Carter
Alicia N Price
Althea Cerka
Amy Hutchings
Amy Johnson
Amy White
Amy Williams
Anastasia Kask
Anda Georgakopoulu
Andrew DiNanno
Andrew Ledford
Andrew Skinner
Angela Boedecker
Anita King
Anna Schmitz
Anna Xie
Anne Farron
Annisa Qurrata Slater
Archie Embleton-Hall
Ariella McNally
Ashley Dennison
Ashley E Wilson
Ashley Eppley
Aubrey Koepke
Avery Wright
Bart Schechinger
Ben Tyreman
Beth Moore
Bethany Morns
Bethany Pearce
Bill Buck
Bill Marx
Billy Edwards
Brenda Culver
Brendan Lynch
Brian Covert
Brian Heath
Brian Horner
Brian Langston
Brittany Knickerbocker

Brooke Fitzwater
Bryan Shickley
Caitlin Teasdale
Callum Pepper
Calum Bray
Carie, care of Lilith Vinter
Carl "Dutch" Dutchin
Carl Potter
Caroline Tran
Carolyn Mennecke
Carys Myfanwy Goddard
Catherine Doyle
Catherine Smith
Catherine Spencer
Catherine Whaley
Cerena Byrd
Charlie Warner
Charlotte Baxter
Charlotte Mann
Charlotte Sutherland
Cheryl Parkhouse
Cheryl Wolder
Chloe Pearce
Chris Ness
Christina Ratzlaff
Christopher Brodigan
Christopher MH Nguyen
Christopher Tate
Claire Fell
Clark Pemberton
Claudia Haschke
Colin Howard
Colleen Ottomano
Cooper Osberg
Courteney Allen
Daniel Berrecloth
Daniel Poulter
Daniel Wilkinson
Danielle Crowley
Darrell Waugh
Dave Hingley
Dave Ladkin
David Lever
David Perez
Dayna Gentieu
Debbie Fischer
Deborah Durbin
Dezirea Beavers
Dulce Gutiérrez
Dung Nguyen
Dylan Atkins
Elaine Wrenn
Elisabeth Fleischmann
Elise Coleman
Elitsa Angelova
Elizabeth Patterson
Elizabeth Stibral
Elizabeth Wallace
Ellen Korver

Emilie Ludwig
Emily Farrah
Emily Hogan
Emily Reppy
Emily Smith
Emma Goddard
Emma J Oebel
Emma Justice
Emmalee Duran
Eoin Finnegan
Eric Streed
Erica Flores
Erica Murphy
Erich Owen
Erin Sweeney
Faith Taylor
Faiz Rehman
Felix Foote
Fiona Chatteur
Fiona James
Focascious Me
Francis Skrzyniarz
Gabriel "RomeTwin" Romer
Gabrielle R Van Deusen
Gemma Holden
Gemma Mains
Genevieve Seldin
Gergely Kocsis
Glenn James
Grace Mutton
Graeme D McGregor
Greg Dorosh
Gretchen Sotebeer
Guy Gardner
Hailey Puckett
Haley Delaney
Halli Lilburn
Hamish Crawford
Hannah Benjestorf
Hannah Ives
Hannah Perry
Hannah Staus
Hannah Street
Hannah Webster
Harrison "Harizonia" Clegg
Harry Draper
Harry Gray
Hayley White
Heather M Weber
Heidi Manley
Helen Brown
Helen Cassin
Hira Malik
Hollie Tatner
Iain McClumpha
Isabel Tippets
Isobel Coffey
Jace Medina
Jacob Heneghan

Jacques De Vere
Jade Musgrave
Jalen Salas
James Bowers
James Clancy
James Gunter
James Morrissey
James Nicol
James O'Neill
James Thresher
Jamie Courtier
Jamie Eve
Jamie Johnson
Jamie Johnston
Jamie Shaw
Jamie White
Janet Yeager
Jared J Margelowsky
Jasmine Harness
Jasmine Penny
Jasmine Schmidt
Jason Fletcher
Jason Usher
Jason Walker
Jay Rogers
Jay Taylor
Jenn Barrett
Jenn Bee
Jenna Mendez
Jennifer Richardson
Jennifer Williams
Jenny Fassenfelt
Jenny Lippmann
Jenny Williams
Jessica Chaleff
Jessica Ward
Jevan Woodrow
Jocelyn Prier
Joe Matt
Joel Small
John Bruce
John Dolan
John Drenkhahn
John Homer
John K Baxter
John Porter
Johnny Waudby
Jon Kearey
Jonathan Dolan
Jonathan Meek
Joni Wood
Joseph Hickey
Joseph Ryder
Joseph Toyer
Joseph Vann
Joshua Kerns
Joshua Ward
Jude Holland
Juliette Ruelland Kennedy

Justin Lee
Karen Samways
Karl Whitmore
Kasey Leslie
Kassandra Alduenda
Katelin & Mikaela Gesslein
Katie Edis
Kayla Matt
Keith Byrne
Kelly Grace Bast
Kelly Müsler
Kent Simpson
Kenzie Glass
Kerenza Lings
Kevin Heasman
Kevin Mains
Kezia Lovell
Kieran Lyman
Kristen Simcox
Kurt Lewis
Kyle Williams
Lacey Valle
Lance Yarema
Larry Walker-Tonks
Laura Inglis
Laurelin Chase
Lauren Brown
Lauriane Ribas Deulofeu
Lauryn Bell
Lawrence Charrett-Dykes
Lee Hamill
Lee Roberts
Leigh Bull
Leilani González-Samalot
Leslie Farrington
Liam Cross
Lindsay Holweger
Lindsey Hitchmough
Livia Mowrer
Lloyd Mills
Louise Veale
Lucas Quinn-Dawes
Lucie Nield
Lucy Crewe
Lukas Berghoff
Lyndon Coleman
Madeline Knapp
Madison Sue Brown
Maja Buckley-Jones
Marcelle Duckett
Maria Rodriguez
Mark Hadlett
Mark Reed
Marla F Fair
Marta England
Martin Ause
Martin Soreide
Mary Meehan
Mary Ogle

Matthew Connolly
Matthew Crooks
Matthew David Curry
Maya Preisler
Megan B Nations
Megan Griffiths
Megan Jewett
Megan Riley
Megan Walker
Melodie Quinton
Melvin Peña
Michael Daws
Michael Maitland
Michalina Turek
Miranda McCarthy
Mitch Wright
Mitchell Smith
Monica Lara
Monika Argenio
Morgan Orr
Morgan Roberts
Moriah Ozberkmen
Moses Alexander Blanco
Nadya Leckenby
Nanci Smith
Nancy Hsu
Naomi Benjestorf
Natalia Jagielska
Natalie Griffiths
Natalie Henderson
Natasha Deacon
Niamh Mackie
Nicholas Martin
Nicole Quezada
Nikki Jonkman
Nikki Martin
Nikole Agnitti
Noel Thomas Simpson
Nola Thepboury
Olga McCall
Oliver Brooks
Olivia Lu
Olivia Nolen
Ozzie Noble
Pat Ennis
Patric Fawcett
Paul Cowan
Paul Mahon
Paul Vought
Paul Watson
Paul Watts
Paula Andrea Guianan
Phil Clements
Phil Potter
Phoebe Rothfeld
Praewa Pitiphat
Rachael Thompson
Rachel, Hayley & John Pope
Ray MacFadyen

Raye Bradford
Rebecca Anniwell
Rebecca Brogan
Rebecca Burton
Riley Dean Creger
Robert Rearick
Robert Steffenino
Robin Hankins
Robyn Mitchell
Ross Bampfylde
Rowan Mallett
Roy Siems, care of Grace L. Gowett
Ruach Ingham
Ruby Thatcher
Ryan Bauscher
Ryan Brennan
Ryan Cluff
Ryan Coster
S T Curd
Sae Wakisaka
Saffron Coulthard
Sam Burgess
Sam Goodchild
Sam R Bentley
Samantha Snyder
Samantha Steele
Sarah Grace Bennett
Sarah Jurgens
Sash Waite
Sasia Marriott-Waite
Saskia Nicholls
Scott DeNino
Sean Hall
Shaleene Lemke
Shaleene Valerie
Shannon Neven
Sherrie Blackwell
Shiela Larson
Simeon Grace
Simon Bromley
Sofia Khalid
Sophie Brudenall
Sophie Cowdrey
Sophie Monks
Stella Small
Stephanie Jackson
Stephen Rowland
Steven Pickford
Sydney Babcock
Sydney Reppy
Sydney Whitcher
Tamara Griner
Tammy Harris
Tasia Rettig
Terri Bone
Tori Hebdon
Valeriane Schmiedt
Vann Storey
Victoria Smith

Victoria Sommer
Wayne W Whited
Wiesenborn11
Willow Topp
Willow Van Rootselaar
Yamil Fayad
Yohann Maucouard
Zakk Haslam
Zarah Tate
Zaylee McLean